Annie Henry

and the
Mysterious Stranger

Adventures of the American Revolution Series

Annie Henry and the Secret Mission

Annie Henry and the Birth of Liberty

Annie Henry and the Mysterious Stranger

Annie Henry and the Redcoats

★ ★ ★ ★ ★ ★ ★ ★ ★ ★ ★ ★ ★ ★ ★ ★ ★ ★
ADVENTURES OF THE AMERICAN REVOLUTION
★ ★ ★ ★ ★ ★ ★ ★ ★ ★ ★ ★ ★ ★ ★ ★ ★ ★

Annie Henry

and the

Mysterious Stranger

Susan Olasky

CROSSWAY BOOKS • WHEATON, ILLINOIS
A DIVISION OF GOOD NEWS PUBLISHERS

Annie Henry and the Mysterious Stranger

Copyright © 1996 by Susan Olasky

Published by Crossway Books
        a division of Good News Publishers
        1300 Crescent Street
        Wheaton, Illinois 60187

Cover illustration: Tom LaPadula

First printing, 1996

Printed in the United States of America

Library of Congress Cataloging-in-Publication Data
Olasky, Susan.
    Annie Henry and the mysterious stranger / Susan Olasky.
        p.   cm. — (Adventures of the American Revolution ; bk. 3)
    Summary: Ten-year-old Annie Henry encounters conflicting values during the year she lives with her father in the Governor's Mansion in Williamsburg.
ISBN 0-89107-907-6
    1. Henry, Annie—Juvenile fiction.   2. Henry, Patrick, 1736–1799—Juvenile fiction. [1. Henry, Annie—Fiction.   2. Henry, Patrick, 1736–1799—Fiction.   3. Fathers and daughters—Fiction. 4. Virginia—History—Revolution, 1775–1783—Fiction.] I. Title. II. Series.
PZ7.0425Am 1996
[Fic]—dc20   96-29070

04		03		02		01		00		99		98		97		96
15	14	13	12	11	10	9	8	7	6	5	4	3	2	1

For
The Hahns: Paul and Fran
Thank you for your faithfulness

CONTENTS

An Accident
9

The Governor's Palace
20

Mistress Hallan's School
28

An Emergency
36

Williamsburg
51

Miss Dandridge
61

The Fair
68

The Race
80

The Maze
91

An Errand of Mercy
99

Annie Comes Back
110

A Christmas Ball
125

A Wedding
137

AN ACCIDENT

FROM HER SEAT IN THE FAMILY CARRIAGE, TWELVE-year-old Annie Henry watched the countryside roll by. The pitted road was, in spots, little more than two worn wagon tracks through the sun-baked fields. On either side were thick stands of corn, wheat, and tobacco. Houses were few and far between and sat back far from the road.

Mile after boring mile the coach lurched along on its way from Scotchtown, the Henrys' home, to Williamsburg, the capital of Virginia. It was early September of 1776 and Patrick Henry, the newly elected governor of Virginia, was returning to the capital after a summer of serious illness. The doctors, uncertain of the diagnosis, had used all the tools available to them. First believing the problem was sick blood, they attached leaches to his skin to suck the "sick blood" out. When he did not get better, they gave him doses of awful medicine. Finally, they threw up their hands and did nothing. At that point, he began recovering.

Now her father was strong enough to travel, but as he lay across from Annie in the coach, she could see the toll his illness had taken. He was thin and pale and even now, after all these weeks, a violent cough sometimes shook his thin body, causing his forehead to bead with sweat. Then Annie would dip her handerchief in the jug of water she carried and mop his fevered brow.

For Annie, this was only her second trip away from Scotchtown, and it was the first time she had ever lived outside rural Hanover County. She left behind an older sister, Patsy, and Patsy's family, as well as three brothers and a younger sister. Thinking about them brought quick tears to her eyes. It would be lonely in Williamsburg, she thought.

For the week prior to leaving, ever since Patsy had decided Annie must go to take care of their father, Annie had felt queasy in her stomach. She knew she wasn't sick, but her stomach felt topsy-turvy, and she had to force herself to eat. Sometimes she woke up at night and could not get back to sleep. It did not help when her older sister tried to comfort her with advice not to worry about tomorrow—today had enough worries of its own.

Now here she was, alone except for a sick father and Phillip, the driver, journeying through this unknown territory. Phillip had assured Patsy that they would stop at an inn to sleep, but Annie still felt uneasy.

She stuck her head outside the carriage window—still no sign of Richmond, their next stop, and the pink horizon behind them warned that sunset was near. Suddenly the carriage jerked forward as the horses galloped crazily from side to side.

"Whoa," the driver shouted as Annie clutched the leather edge of her seat. Across from her, Patrick Henry's head bumped the wood-paneled wall of the carriage, jerking him awake.

"Runaway horses," Annie whispered.

"Pray, Annie," he whispered, closing his eyes.

For several desperate minutes the horses ran out of control while the driver struggled bravely to halt them. Then, just as suddenly, the carriage stopped, shuddering violently before tilting dangerously to one side.

Inside the coach, the wicker picnic basket slid across the floor. Annie screamed as her father rolled off his seat, hitting his head sharply on the floor. She scrambled to his side, holding her breath as the coach rocked violently. He appeared dazed but was able to lift himself back onto his seat.

"Are you all right, Father?" she whispered.

He nodded his head, but then closed his eyes and seemed to drift off to sleep. Annie sat there anxiously. Should she stay near him, or climb out of the carriage and look after Phillip? She sat still for a moment, thinking through her options, but the deepening shadows told her the sun was setting rapidly, and soon they would be in darkness. At least Annie could light the carriage lanterns before that happened.

Because the carriage was on its side, one door was pinned shut by the ground. Slowly she inched her way across the seat until she could reach the handle of the other door. She turned it and pushed the door open. Then, putting her hands on both sides of the opening, she pulled herself though. From her perch on the edge, she leapt to the ground, holding her breath as the carriage rocked and then settled back into its unsafe position.

"Phillip?" she called.

There was no answer, and Annie feared the worst. She circled the carriage and saw, lying against a tree, the shaken but conscious driver. He was rubbing his forehead, where she could see a black-and-blue lump already forming.

"What happened?" she asked.

"I don't know. Those crazy horses . . . I don't know what spooked them. It almost sounded like gunshot, but it couldn't have been. Not way out here. Anyway, they've gone and broke the wheel clear in two. Let's see about the axle."

Bending down, he looked under the carriage. Then standing up, he brushed the dirt off his hands. "Axle looks fine," he announced. "That's luck for you."

"Or God's providence," the girl whispered. "Can you fix the wheel?"

"There's a spare on the back," he said. "But I'll need help to raise the carriage. You aren't big enough, and your father isn't strong enough. We may have to wait until day-light, then I can ride for help."

At those words, Annie let the tears she had been try-ing desperately to hold back, flow. The driver reached out awkwardly to pat her arm. "Don't cry, Miss Annie," he pleaded. "We'll be safe here. Why, we must not be more than an hour from Richmond. There won't be no trou-ble, and you can sleep comfortably in the carriage. Please don't cry."

Phillip's words shamed the girl into silence. But she trembled when she thought of spending the night out in the dark countryside.

"What about Father?" she asked.

"Was he injured?" Phillip asked, a worried expression on his face.

She bit her lip uncertainly. "He banged his head hard, and then drifted off to sleep," she said.

"Sleep is the best thing," Phillip nodded in reply, relieved that his poor driving hadn't injured the governor.

"Couldn't we light the lanterns?" she pleaded as she looked around at the deepening shadows.

"Sure. That's a good idea. Then I'll unharness one of the horses and ride back to those woods and gather some wood. We'll need it for a fire."

"But," Annie protested, "you wouldn't leave me here alone," she said. "Why do we need a fire? It's warm out."

"You ask too many questions," Phillip said, annoyed at her chatter. "Let me go to work. Without a fire, who knows what kind of animals we'll have creeping about."

Annie bit back her reply. She wouldn't let him see how frightened she was. "At least leave me the musket," she said.

After he finished lighting the candle inside one of the carriage lamps, he lowered the glass. The flame flickered, then glowed. Its soft light brightened the area around the carriage, putting Annie a bit at ease. She watched as he unhitched the horse, saddled it, and tied the other lamp to its saddle. "I won't be long," he said.

She carried the musket over to a tree about twenty feet from the road. Its low-hanging branches made it perfect for climbing, and she tied her long skirts out of the way and proceeded to scamper up. By now it was pitch dark, except near the carriage where the lantern softly glowed. Annie felt fairly safe in her hiding place. She kept her eyes on the road Phillip had taken, wishing he would return.

She must have dozed because the sudden sound of horse hooves jerked her to attention. Could it be Phillip already? she wondered. Peering through the gloom, her eyes picked out a heavyset figure on a dark horse. It couldn't be Phillip, she thought. He's not nearly that big.

She drew the musket a bit closer to her. "I never loaded it," she groaned. Had Phillip done so? She watched as the rider got off his horse some distance from the carriage. He walked silently toward the disabled carriage, looking about him secretively. He means no good, Annie thought, pulling back against the trunk of the tree.

"Please, let Father not wake up," she begged. "Let him be quiet."

In the light of the lantern Annie thought she saw a glint of silver. Was it a knife? She held her breath, uncertain what to do. In the dim light she knew she had little chance to shoot the man even if the musket were loaded. It would be better to wait until she knew her father was in danger before even trying to shoot. So she held still.

Closer the man crept toward the carriage until he came to a stop before a dark shape on the ground. Then, as the girl watched, he pulled a long dagger out of its sheath and bent down toward the shape. She leaned forward in her branch trying to see better what he was doing. There was a tearing sound as the man struggled with the dark form. The trunk, Annie thought. It had come off the carriage during the accident. She could see now that he had forced open the lid and was rummaging about, throwing clothes this way and that as he searched for anything of value. Several times he paused, looked around and listened intently before continuing his silent work. When he had finished at the trunk, he rose and began to walk over to the carriage where Patrick Henry slept.

Annie's finger tightened on the trigger. The heavy weapon trembled in her sweaty hand, and she prayed that she wouldn't have to use it. When the man reached the carriage, he started for the door. Abruptly, though, he turned and pulled the lantern from its hook. Using the light, he returned to the trunk and continued his search. She watched him pocket several small items. Money probably, and maybe her father's silver buttons. When he finished, he once again crept toward the carriage, carrying the lantern in his hand.

The wind blew and a broken branch fell from Annie's tree. The sound it made as it rustled through the limbs and crashed to the ground startled the girl. The highwayman paused and stared directly at her hiding place. She froze, certain he could see her. As he stared, he held the lantern a little higher so that Annie, for the first time, caught a good glimpse of his face. He was a heavy man, with a fleshy face and thick neck. His small, deepset eyes were almost swallowed up by his puffy eyelids.

For a minute the two were frozen in a silence. The stillness was broken by the sound of Phillip's horse. Louder and louder came the hoofbeats as the horse drew nearer to the coach. Silently—and quickly for such a big man—the highwayman rose and ran to his horse. He seemed to melt into the darkness, disappearing without a trace, with only the sound of his retreating animal.

"Who goes there?" Phillip shouted when he heard the other rider. He rode into the circle of light and seemed to hesitate. Should he follow the highwayman?

When Annie saw that it was Phillip, she shimmied down the trunk of the tree, ignoring the pain as the rough trunk scraped her legs. "Phillip," she screamed as she ran toward him. By this time he had dismounted his horse and was examining the mess before him. There lay the ransacked trunk with the broken lock. Shattered lantern glass glittered on the ground.

"What happened here?" Phillip asked, his face white. "Your Father . . . ?"

"It was a highwayman," Annie whispered in a trembling voice. "I hid in a tree."

"Let's check on the governor."

Together they walked to the carriage, and Phillip lifted the slender girl until she could peek through the door. Her father still slept, his chest gently rising and falling.

"Now tell me about this man," Phillip asked, looking about nervously. "Was it one or a gang?"

"Just one," Annie said. "He tethered his horse a ways from the carriage and walked over. Then he broke open the lock and took some things from Father's trunk."

"Did he have a gun?"

"Not in his hand," she answered. "Only a dagger. What do you think he would have done if you hadn't come back?" she asked.

"Only God knows," he answered. "But I wish we could go on tonight," Phillip added nervously. "I wouldn't have expected highwaymen to be operating so close to Richmond. Have we lost all respect for the law?"

"At least let us make a fire," the frightened girl begged. "I have had enough surprises tonight. I don't want to meet a bear."

Immediately Phillip set to work building a fire, and

soon the flame burned brightly, sending little sparks drifting up into the sky. Although the night was hot, Annie shivered. Even the hot fire couldn't seem to warm her.

Looking up from his work, Phillip shouted at the girl. "Get back from there. All we need is for your long skirts to catch fire."

She drew back and looked at the driver apologetically. She knew he felt an extra measure of concern because she was there.

"I want you to get back in the carriage," he said after he had picked up the scattered remnants from the trunk. "Your father will feel better knowing that you are safe inside."

With his help, she climbed back into the carriage. Her father roused himself momentarily. "Why haven't we fixed the wheel?" he mumbled.

"It's too heavy for Phillip to manage alone," she answered. "We'll sleep here tonight, and he'll get help in the morning. Richmond isn't far." Annie spoke soothingly, knowing that her father was still disoriented from the accident. "Sleep now, and in the morning we'll be able to continue our journey to Williamsburg."

Although her father soon slept, Annie could not. She tossed and turned on the uncomfortably tilted seat. Sometimes she felt herself drifting off, but then the howl of a wolf or the hooting of an owl startled her awake. Once she peered out of the carriage and saw Phillip on guard, puffing his pipe and holding the musket on his lap.

☆

It was the sound of birds singing that Annie heard first. She opened her eyes sleepily and looked about the cramped carriage. Her father was sitting up on his seat. Although he looked gray and weak, she was glad to see him awake. Before she could speak, though, she heard the sound of horses. Holding her breath, the girl put her finger to her mouth in a warning to her father to be quiet.

"Hello," a voice called out. "Do you need help there?"

It was a friendly greeting and Annie relaxed, but her father shook his head. Even highwaymen could pretend to be friendly. Why didn't Phillip answer?

She heard the scuff of a boot on the dry ground and then a hearty laugh. "Startled you, didn't I," the stranger said. "I saw the smoke from your fire and thought I might get some food. I didn't expect to be put to work this early, but I'm glad to help."

From Phillip came a groggy response, and Annie guessed that he had been found sleeping.

"I'm Spencer Roane," the stranger said. Annie saw her father smile.

"It's okay, daughter," he said. "Mr. Roane is a law student in Williamsburg. "We'll be safe now."

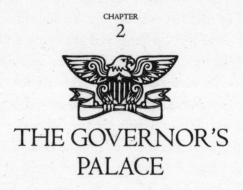

THE GOVERNOR'S PALACE

WITH MR. ROANE'S HELP PHILLIP WAS ABLE TO FIX THE wheel, and soon the carriage was on its way. When the law student realized who was inside, he became excited. Riding his horse alongside the coach, he leaned down and talked to the governor.

"We are so glad that you are well," he said. "There has been worry that you might not come back. Many, including Mr. Jefferson and Mr. Madison, feared that without your leadership, the factions would not hold together."

Annie listened to them with one ear. She was glad to see her father sitting up and taking an interest in the world about him. Talking politics with this young man seemed to energize him. The two men ignored her, so she turned her attention to the countryside. From the window, she caught glimpses of the river—probably the James—and saw the tips of white sails against the blue autumn sky.

War seemed far off in this peaceful setting. But then she remembered the highwayman and realized that it wasn't. She listened to Mr. Roane's news.

"I've been riding from Philadelphia," he said. "The news from New York is not good. General Washington has been fighting valiantly against General Howe on Long Island. But Howe's massive numbers forced Washington to retreat to Manhattan. They believe further attacks by the British are coming."

"How are his troops holding out?" Henry asked.

"There are many deserters—boys who joined the militia for adventure but were not prepared to fight," Mr. Roane replied. "Others have already fulfilled their terms and are ready to leave. If we don't send Washington more soldiers and food, and the clothing to supply them, we will surely lose this war."

The words were grim, and the weight of them turned the mood somber as the carriage rolled into the outskirts of Williamsburg. Once into the safety of the town, Mr. Roane said good-bye and spurred his horse on, eager to get to the Raleigh tavern to spread the news.

By now they had entered the town, past the redbrick buildings of William and Mary College, past the Bruton Parish Church. The carriage slowed and turned. Patrick Henry said, "Look out your window."

Annie looked. In front of her was a long tree-lined green. Looming at the end of it was a large two-story brick mansion behind a tall brick wall. "That is our home, Annie," her weary father said.

Annie gazed at the mansion in silence while wondering, "Would Williamsburg ever be home?"

☆

When Annie awoke the next morning, she was in a bed in a strange but beautiful room. She looked about at the green-flowered, paper-covered walls, and at the three tall windows that lined one side. From her canopy hung green and purple flowered curtains, which matched the coverlet on her bed.

A wardrobe filled one wall, and a small table with two chairs sat in a corner. Annie climbed down from the tall bed, using the step stool that stood next to it. She opened the wardrobe and saw that all her dresses had been hung neatly. On the washstand was a pitcher of water. She stuck her finger in; it was hot. Pouring a bit into the wash bowl, Annie washed the road dust off her face and neck. She brushed her hair and tied a ribbon in it.

After dressing, Annie opened the drapes and saw that the windows all overlooked the green. From her perch she could see the comings and goings of all the people who had business at the governor's palace.

Eager to explore the rest of the house, Annie opened her door and slipped out into the hallway. Her father's room was across the hall, but Annie didn't want to bother him yet. Instead, she ran outside where she found the kitchen and scullery. There slaves were already busy washing dishes. There was a bath house and a smokehouse, and a livery where two men were already working on the damaged carriage. Smoke billowed from the chimney of the blacksmith's shop. Behind the walls of the Palace, a virtual city existed. Almost everything the governor needed was produced on his own land.

Slaves watched the young girl curiously as she ran from place to place. Children giggled and pointed at the new resident. There was so much to explore that Annie wished her brothers were there to enjoy it with her. She knew they would like playing hide-and-seek in the wine cellar. From behind the kitchen, she caught a glimpse of the canal and knew that William and John would be fishing this minute if they were here.

A grumbling in her stomach led Annie back indoors. She found that a table had been set for her in the dining room, and she ate breakfast alone, something she had never done at Scotchtown. Even though she didn't have to fight her hungry brothers for the last biscuit, Annie found her food strangely tasteless. "I'd rather have less and be with my family," she said to herself, "than to have all these riches and be alone."

☆

"I won't go!" Annie said. "I didn't come to Williamsburg to go to school."

From the bed where Patrick Henry lay came a deep chuckle.

"But, Father, I've seen those city girls at church. They are sillier than our cows back home, and to think of having to spend every day at school with them . . ."

Annie sat down on one of the chairs that had been left behind when the last royal governor, Lord Dunmore, had escaped out the backdoor of the Palace, fearing for his life. Dunmore had the misfortune to be the king's representative in 1776, just at the time that American colonists were ready to throw out British rule.

Annie's father sighed. "Maybe I should have left you home," he muttered.

"But, Father," the girl protested, "you know you were to weak to come back to Williamsburg alone. Patsy and the doctor wouldn't have stood for it. But they warned me how stubborn you could be."

Another chuckle came from the area of the canopied bed on which the sick governor lay.

A week had gone by since the Henrys' arrival in Williamsburg. From the first, Patrick Henry had talked about sending his daughter to school. But Annie had protested. Now, however, thinking her father's mood had softened, the girl leaned forward to state what she thought was her best argument against going. "I can't very well take care of you if I'm at school all day, can I?" she asked, as if that settled the matter. Leaning back in the chair, she crossed her arms and waited for her father to give in.

But when the governor spoke, it was only to say, "Well, lass, the matter's already settled. I've paid Mistress Hallan your first month's tuition. You start on Monday." Before Annie could protest, her father yawned. "Not now, Annie," he said, "I have to rest. Please close the door behind you."

Annie stared at her father, not really believing that the argument was over just like that. Without a word, she rose from the chair and left the room, banging the door closed behind her. She stood for a minute just on the other side of the door, debating whether it was worth trying one more time to get her father to relent. She stood in a large open room at the top of the stairs, where royal governors had entertained visitors. It was a gloomy place, with dark walls that matched Annie's foul mood.

The floor smelled faintly of lye soap, and wet patches near the walls gave evidence that it had just been scrubbed. The girl walked across the room to the door of her own bedroom, scuffing the soft leather soles of her shoes against the floor's planks.

Coming to Williamsburg to nurse an ill father had been one thing; going to school with city-bred ladies was another. She stormed into her bedroom and threw open her wardrobe doors. The sight did nothing to cheer her up. There hung the little frocks she had worn for years at Scotchtown. But now she saw them with Williamsburg eyes, and she knew they were unfashionable. If she were to wear them to school, she would be marked as a baby and a country girl. Proud as she was, Annie didn't think she could bear the ridicule.

Tears of frustration welled in her eyes. From the Henrys' high-backed church pew, Annie had seen the young ladies in their hoop skirts and satin dresses. They seemed silly, and Annie didn't want anything to do with them. And most especially, she didn't want to go to school with them.

She rubbed away the tears savagely. "You're twelve years old," she said to herself. "Too old to cry." Just then, outside the door, Annie heard footsteps. Smoothing her hair she turned to face the door, trying to rub away every trace of tears. There was a knock and then Mr. Goodacre, the butler, said, "Mr. Thomas Jefferson is here to see Governor Henry. Is your father well enough for visitors?"

Annie opened the door. "My father was just taking a nap," she said. "Perhaps it would be best if you told people that Father would only receive callers in the morning. He seems much stronger then."

With a nod and a bow, Mr. Goodacre turned and went back downstairs. Annie slid quietly across the floor and leaned over the bannister to get a glimpse of the famous visitor. In the reception room downstairs, the tall and handsome Mr. Jefferson talked earnestly to Mr. Goodacre. As Annie leaned over to hear what they said, her foot caught the hem of her dress and she stumbled. Catching herself, the girl looked down just in time to meet Thomas Jefferson's gaze. He winked, before turning to leave.

With cheeks blazing, Annie rushed back to her room. It was bad enough to be clumsy and almost fall down the stairs. But to do it when a man like Thomas Jefferson was watching. And for him to know that she had been eavesdropping. Annie shuddered and burrowed her head under her pillow.

MISTRESS HALLAN'S SCHOOL

MONDAY DAWNED BRIGHT AND COLD. ANNIE HAD wanted an earthquake or a tornado—anything to keep school from meeting. But she was disappointed. Now she was on her way to the dreaded destination. Under the yellow canopy formed by the towering catalpa trees that lined the Palace green, Annie shuffled her way to Mistress Hallan's. Her boots kicked up the dried leaves that had gathered in the gutter along the side of the road, and her thoughts turned toward school. Even thinking about entering the strange classroom set Annie's stomach churning. She thought for one panicked moment that she was going to be sick right there on the Green. But the queasiness passed, and the girl plodded on toward her destination, her shoes clip-clopping along the cobblestone road.

When she reached the corner of Duke of Gloucester Street, Annie looked wistfully back at the Palace. No familiar face stood at the gate watching and waving. With resignation, she crossed the busy street, careful to step around the piles of horse manure that dirtied the road. Mistress Hallan's little house was on Queen Street, just around the corner from Duke of Gloucester, no more than three minutes away, but Annie managed to walk so slowly, with so little purpose, that she didn't arrive for fifteen minutes and was late.

She knocked hesitantly and then waited. Eventually the door was opened by a maid who silently ushered the nervous girl into the parlor. In a minute, Annie was joined by a stern-looking woman who looked pointedly at the mantel clock. "Ten-fifteen," the woman said. "My school is run on time, even for the governor's daughter."

Annie blushed and whispered an apology. The sour-faced teacher nodded and led her charge into the school room. Five pairs of eyes looked up as Annie entered the room. She knew right away that she was all wrong for this school. She looked like a country cousin amidst all the city finery. Though she had thought it wouldn't bother her, she found that it did. She was suddenly self-concious of the cut of her dress and the style of her hair.

For a minute she wished she could disappear, but then she heard a soft voice in her head telling her to stand up straight and be proud. She was the governor's daughter. So Annie did. She smiled stiffly, the way she had practiced in her bedroom whenever she imagined herself a queen, until each one of the girls was forced to smile back.

Mistress Hallan interrupted this silent ritual by say-ing, "Let me introduce the other young ladies. Letitia Gray," she said pointing to a pretty girl with her hair piled six inches higher than her forehead. "Let me introduce the governor's daughter, Annie Henry." The girl nodded and Annie winced, fearing the mass of hair would fall into her face. "Next to Letitia is her cousin Diana North," the teacher added, as a white-capped young lady in a satin sack dress looked up. "Diana is related to a cousin of the king, isn't that so, Diana?" The girl nodded, barely able to restrain the pride that showed on her face. "And this is Grace Jones," the teacher went on. "Grace's father is a very prominent attorney in Williamsburg," she added with an anxious smile at the tall girl who nodded at Annie.

After the first three girls were introduced, Annie noted a change in the teacher's attitude. "This is Virginia Galt," she said as she pointed at a pale girl with mousy hair tucked into a white cap. "Her father has the apothe-cary shop. And this is Kate Marsh." Kate kept her eyes on the table, and Annie thought she heard snickers before the teacher shushed them away. "Hush, girls. Your parents don't expect you to go about snickering."

The other girls settled back to work, and Annie removed her own ink and quill from her satchel. As she readied her paper, she observed the others secretly. All the girls except Kate and Virginia were dressed in fine gowns with hoops, and lace on the sleeves. All the girls wore white caps, except for Letititia, who wore pearls tucked into her tower of hair.

As Annie observed the girls out of the corner of her eye, she found that Diana was watching her. Embarrassed, she brought her attention back to her work. She carefully dipped her quill in her ink well and began writing out one of the *Poor Richard* sayings by Ben Franklin: "A stitch in time saves nine."

Over and over each girl formed the words until Mistress Hallan was satisfied that their letters were perfect. Annie had no patience for this kind of careful work. She worked hurriedly, smearing her still wet letters with the side of her hand so that she would have to start again. Sometimes she loaded too much ink on her pen and created an unsightly blob on her paper. The other girls worked quietly and neatly, and Annie could feel her face get hot as she struggled vainly to get one page done without error. "I guess country girls have no reason to learn to write," she heard Letty whisper to Diana. Then Diana smiled sweetly to Annie and said out loud, "Don't worry. By the time Mistress Hallan is finished with you, you'll be able to write a beautiful letter. My father already lets me write all his correspondence. But then, the governor probably doesn't need any help from his daughter."

Annie was thinking of a reply when Mistress Hallan interrupted and announced it was time for tea. The girls moved to the dining room where a pot of herbal tea sat on a sideboard along with a tray of small sandwiches and sweet cakes, which a maid served to each young lady. Even during tea, the lessons continued.

"Ladies, when inviting someone of your own station to supper, it is polite to say, 'Sir, you shall oblige me very much if you will do me the honor to take my poor dinner with me.'"

When Mistress Hallan had finished, Kate asked shyly, "But why don't we say it plainly, ma'am?"

Diana and Letty, who had been whispering together, looked with exasperation at Kate. "Because we are not plain, Kate," Letty said primly, while Diana giggled behind her hand.

Annie bit her tongue. She wasn't going to get into fights today, but she determined to become friends with Kate, even if it cost her the company of these fine young ladies. Mistress Hallan turned to Kate and said, "These are rules for polite company. You may never need to use them." Kate blushed a deep red, and the other girls tittered, but the tutor seemed unaware that she had slighted one of her students.

For the next several minutes the girls ate the meal spread before them, conciously keeping one hand in their laps and saying the many polite phrases Mistress Hallan had taught them. When the teacher left the room for a moment, Letitia stood up, glancing around to make sure she would not be overheard by the mistress.

"Young ladies," she trilled in a poor imitation of the teacher, "bite not thy bread, but break it, but not with slovenly fingers," she said, as she imitated someone stuffing food in her mouth.

"Shh. Sit down, Letty, before the old biddy comes back," Diana hissed. But the girl wasn't ready to give up her stage.

"Spit not, cough not, nor blow thy nose at thy table if it may be avoided," she said, daintily wiping her nose with her handkerchief as the other girls roared with laughter.

Grace took up where Letty left off. "Stuff not thy mouth so as to fill thy cheeks," she said, puffing out her cheeks like a little chipmunk. "Be content with smaller mouthfuls." With those words she turned and stared meaningfully at Annie who had just put a small cake in her mouth. All the girls giggled, while Annie tried to swallow the offending sweet. Just then, footsteps on the wood floor sent Grace back to her chair.

The girls were choking back laughter when Mistress Hallan returned. Kate, whose back was to the teacher, didn't see her enter the room. She caught the teacher's wrath. "Kate, it is low to carry on like that at table," the teacher said with a prim scowl. Poor Kate blushed scarlet again, and Annie squirmed.

With relief, Annie left school at the end of the day. The minute they had been excused, Virginia and Kate hurried out the door. Annie hurried after them but was interrupted by a voice behind her.

"Why are you rushing so?" Grace called.

"I'm just glad to be done, and I do want to see Father," Annie answered.

"Don't rush off. We usually go buy a sweet and gossip for a bit. Will you come?"

Annie could see Letty and Diana standing a few yards away. She felt torn. She knew she should get home to see her father, but she wanted desperately to go. "I guess I had better not," she said regretfully. "Father has been sick, and I should get home to him."

"Oh, come," Grace urged. "Your father has servants who can see after his health."

It took only a little urging for Annie to relent. "I'll come," she said. "But I must not stay long."

The girls giggled as they walked along Duke of Gloucester Street. "Why don't Kate and Virginia come?" Annie asked.

"They are lucky to get out of work at all, even for school," Grace said with a laugh. "You should see that Old Mrs. Wythe. She keeps a tight reign on Kate. That's why that girl is such a goose. She's afraid her own shadow might jump out and bite her."

"My father says that old Mr. Galt is as tightfisted a man as he ever knew," Letty added. "It's a wonder he lets Virginia go to school. He's certainly not going to let her have a pence to go for a sweet." Annie was about to tell how she had worked at a tavern the previous summer when Grace interrupted. "Work is so boring to think about. I'm grateful for servants. My mother says that my job is to catch a good husband."

That set all the girls to giggling, and soon they were talking about dresses and dances. It wasn't until the church bell chimed that Annie realized an hour had passed. By then a fall breeze had begun to whip up the leaves along the gutter and send them scudding across the street. Regretfully, Annie looked at the darkening sky. "I really must be going," she said.

"Come again tomorrow," they called out after her.

"I will," she agreed, as she quickened her pace toward home.

AN EMERGENCY

FOR SEVERAL WEEKS, ANNIE WENT BACK AND FORTH to school. She fell into the rhythms of Mistress Hallan's classroom and learned what was expected of her. And she also learned the rules of Williamsburg society. It was clear that Grace was the leader at Mistress Hallan's. The other girls tried to dress like her. They put on bored faces when Grace was bored. And when Grace suggested a prank, all the girls went along.

Because Annie was the governor's daughter, Grace didn't tease her as much as she teased Kate or Virginia, but Diana and Letty never failed to make snide remarks about her clothes. One day Annie arrived at school just as Kate was setting up her desk. She put her small jar of ink on the table and placed her quill carefully alongside her one piece of paper. Annie knew that Kate did not have much extra paper because it was so expensive. Her work was done painstakingly, so that every line was used and none wasted.

Once her table was in order, Kate went into the parlor to wait for the other girls. In the meantime, Annie set up her own table, laying out her ink and quill pen. As she worked, Grace rushed through the back door, her long cape flapping behind her. Setting her satchel on the floor, she proceeded to remove from it two jars of ink. One she placed at her own seat, but the other she put at Kate's. Then she removed Kate's own jar.

Annie gave her a puzzled look but said nothing. Maybe Grace is giving Kate some better ink, she thought. Everyone knew that Kate made her own ink with water, ink powder, and vinegar to make it go further. Putting the matter out of her head, Annie followed Grace into the parlor where they had morning prayer and Bible reading.

Several times Annie saw Grace exchange secretive glances with Diana and Letty. When Bible reading had ended, the girls went into the classroom, filing through the doorway one at a time because their hoop skirts filled it completely. Annie dipped her own pen in the ink and began writing, carefully blotting the wet ink so that it would not get on her hand and white cuff.

The other girls seemed strangely quiet, and when Annie looked up she saw them waiting as Kate dipped her pen into her ink. She turned to see what was so interesting. Kate seemed to be unaware of the attention. Carefully, she pressed her quill to paper. With horror,

Annie watched as a stain, which looked like blood, spread from the sharpened point of her quill. Kate screamed and threw down her quill, splattering the blood red ink all over the table. Grace's shoulders twitched and the other girls struggled to hold back giggles. Then Kate burst into tears.

The noise brought Mistress Hallan, who had been in the parlor, rushing into the room. "What's going on here," she demanded as she saw Kate crying before her ruined work and the other girls sitting in innocent silence.

"There's blood in my ink," Kate sobbed.

"Oh, nonsense," Mistress Hallan said after gingerly picking up the spoiled paper and sniffing the red stain. "It's nothing but berry juice. Can't you even make a decent pot of ink?"

"But my ink is black," Kate said with an injured expression. "This isn't my ink."

"And just whose is it?" Mistress Hallan answered. "You've made a mess not only of your own paper but of my table as well." The teacher began scrubbing the red liquid off her table, muttering under her breath in a voice loud enough for them all to hear, "This is what comes from trying to be generous."

As the mess was cleaned, Kate sat sobbing in her chair. The other girls looked at her awkwardly until Diana snapped, "Hush, girl. Do you want Mistress Hallan to send you home? Then what would Mrs. Wythe say?" The threat of being sent home was enough to silence the girl.

Amidst the confusion, Annie watched Grace who

never let on that she knew about the ink bottles. She helped wipe up the mess, patted Kate sympathetically, and made herself useful, until Annie began to doubt what she had seen. Over and over again she played back the incident, trying to make sense of it. Meanwhile, her own work suffered because she couldn't concentrate. Mistress Hallan would have thrown up her arms in complete exasperation if Annie hadn't been the daughter of the governor.

With relief, she gathered up her belongings at the end of the day and rushed to be the first one out the door and up the street. Even though she heard her name being called, Annie didn't stop and answer but walked as briskly as she could towards home. When she entered through the gate, she finally relaxed. At least at the Palace she could count on people behaving normally. Because she didn't want to see anyone, especially not the butler who seemed to stand sentry near the front door, Annie crept around the side of the house until she heard voices and laughter. There, under an enormous magnolia tree, sat Patrick Henry, his head covered with a silk turban, looking a bit like a scrawny buzzard. But what caught Annie's attention was the fact that her father wasn't alone.

At his side sat a young woman who, at that moment, bent forward and whispered something to him. He threw his head back and laughed so heartily that Annie feared he might have a fit. She had never seen her father behave that way. But then, as the girl watched from behind the tree, the strange woman reached out her hand and touched his arm. And he kissed her hand. It was so unexpected that Annie almost cried aloud, but she caught herself just in time.

Dropping her satchel on the lawn and kicking off her shoes and stockings, the girl ran past the kitchen to where the garden still flourished, despite the changing weather. Rows of potatoes and sweet potatoes, cabbages and brussel sprouts, herbs and other late crops grew on the terraced hillside. Annie skipped down the slope until she came to the pathway that meandered around the banks of a canal.

The trees still wore their fall colors. They rose up in orange and yellow splendor, and their reflections were caught in the calm waters of the canal. Several swans swam toward Annie, expecting to be fed, but she hadn't brought any crumbs with her. Shuffling her feet through the dry leaves, she walked along the bank, stopping now and then to pick up a pebble and try to skip it across the water's glassy surface.

Before too long she was out of sight of the Palace and enveloped in the woods and gardens that bordered the canal. As long as Annie stayed on this side of the canal, it wasn't possible to get lost. The gardens—and even the woods here—were tame compared to the countryside around Scotchtown. This was the governor's land—and Annie knew it would be a very bold trespasser or poacher who would dare to come on the governor's property.

Just like at home, Annie found the woods to be a comfort. She let herself be soothed by the sound of the wind and the chattering of the squirrels. She followed one path after another, until she was quite confused about where she was. There was a wide path that led from the canal to the side of a hill. There, Annie found the icehouse buried in the hillside. The path had been made by servants dragging heavy blocks of ice from the canal in winter to the small building. From the top of the hill, Annie looked down onto a maze sculpted out of boxwood plants, and beyond that she could see the formal gardens nearer the Palace.

Surrounded by the great beauty of the gardens, Annie felt all alone. She had yet to make a real friend in Williamsburg. In fact, the longer she stayed, the less she understood. And now her father, the one person she had thought she could count on, was acting odd. It was too much for the girl to bear. Suddenly, she wanted nothing more than to go riding.

Running back to the house, Annie rushed upstairs and put on a pair of sturdy boots. The sun was low in the sky, so she wrapped a cape around herself and went back down to the stable. The governor had many horses to choose from, but Annie asked the groom to saddle a gentle one. She didn't want to be bucked off.

He put her saddle on a small bay mare and helped the young girl mount. "I'd keep off the streets, Miss Annie," he said. "You aren't used to all the traffic."

Annie nodded as she walked the horse to the gate.

They picked their way over the cobblestone road at a leisurely pace. Annie didn't want to run until she reached an open field. Once there, she gave the mare its head. For the first time in a long time, Annie felt the rush of the wind against her cheek. She bent low over the horse's neck, letting the animal's warmth warm her skin. Finally, she pulled up on the reins until the horse stopped. She let him graze for a minute while she looked around.

Across the field, Annie saw the college. The tents she had seen when they had driven into town still stood forlornly against the darkening sky. Annie urged the horse on toward them, curious to see what the army looked like up close. As they drew near, she could see young men squatting near their fires, looking tired and dirty. There were no uniforms to be seen, and the men looked too scraggly to be of much use to General Washington or anyone else.

"Hello, ma'am," a young soldier said, lifting his tricorner hat as Annie rode by. She smiled and waved at all the boys who looked so much like her brothers. Some played cards, and a few were tossing a dagger into the ground. A bit away from the crowd, a group of boys about her age were marching. Their leader bellowed at a fellow who lagged behind his companions, "Monroe, James Monroe." Annie watched with amusement as the slowpoke ran to keep up.

She made her way around the outskirts of the camp where she was overtaken by a young man on a horse.

"This may not be the safest place for you to be riding," he said.

"I wasn't meaning any harm," Annie answered apologetically, looking up at him. He looked familiar.

"Of course not. But an army camp is not the place for a young lady, especially one alone. May I help you back to your home?" he asked.

"No, I'm fine," Annie answered, puzzling over where she'd seen him before. "The Governor's Palace is not far, and I have plenty of light. But thank you."

"So you are the governor's daughter?" he said.

"I'm Annie Henry," she answered.

"I'm James Madison," he said, tipping his tricorner hat. "Your father and I have often been allies."

Annie smiled in recognition. Under Mr. Madison's watchful glance she urged her horse back to the Palace grounds. By the time she reached the stable, the sun was setting and a sharp north wind had begun to blow.

☆

That night seemed long to Annie. She had barely spoken to her father at dinner because he seemed distracted. And she had tossed and turned all night, finding it hard to sleep. In the early morning she drifted off and then slept too long. When she woke up, she saw that it was late and she would be tardy unless she hurried. There was no time to say good-bye to her father. Snatching up her satchel, she ran out the gate and up the Palace green to

Duke of Gloucester Street. In the churchyard, a deacon talked to a man dressed in black as several slaves labored to dig a grave in the hard soil.

When she arrived at the teacher's house, Annie found the school mistress all aflutter. She looked nothing like the efficient teacher of the day before. Today her cotton cap sat crookedly and from under it sprang several unruly clumps of hair.

Kate stood forlornly in a corner, and Annie felt a twinge of guilt as she remembered Grace's cruel practical joke. Because she felt guilty, she didn't go talk to her. Instead, she stood in another corner waiting for the other girls to arrive. It wasn't long before Letty and Diana swept into the room.

"Whatever is the matter?" Diana asked as she saw her teacher's disarray. "Is it the gout?" Letty asked, not knowing what gout was, but knowing that it made her father terrible to be around.

"Probably dispepsia," Diana whispered.

For some reason, that set the two girls into a fit of giggles, but Mistress Hallan didn't seem to notice.

Letty joined Annie in the corner, but Diana took Mistress Hallan by the arm and urged her to take a seat. "I wish Grace was here," she said. "She'd know what to do.

"Mother always has a cup of tea when she swoons," Letty said. "Why not get some tea?"

Diana looked around for the maid and said sharply,

"Please bring a cup of herb tea to your mistress. She is not feeling well."

By the time the maid had brought the much-needed refreshment, Grace had arrived. She immediately took things in hand. "What troubles your mistress?" she asked the maid.

"Mistress got a letter this morning and has been acting flighty ever since," the maid answered.

Grace knelt by the teacher's chair. "What has happened to disturb you so?"

"I'm worried," the woman said, barely holding back the tears. "I've had a letter saying that my mother and sister have come down with the pox. They refused vaccination last year, and now they are both at death's door. I must go to them. Duty requires it. But I don't like to leave my responsibilities here," she whispered, barely able to restrain the tears.

Grace nodded her head. "Of course you must go home," she said. "We don't need to have school until you get back."

The other girls looked at each other, all thinking the same thing: vacation.

Immediately, Diana agreed, "You must go to your family in their time of need. Wouldn't you agree, Letty?"

Letty had joined Diana at the teacher's side, and the two girls both nodded their heads vigorously, Letty adding, "We'll miss you terribly, of course, but there is no other solution. Of course you must go." Then, turning to Annie, she said with a bright smile, "Wouldn't you agree?"

Annie was glad that school would be canceled, but the feeling was followed quickly by shame. How could she rejoice in Mistress Hallan's sadness?

With the six girls twittering about, it seemed certain that someone would faint. But Grace took control of the situation.

"Since there is no school today or in the coming weeks, there is no reason for you all to stay here. Letty and Diana, why don't you leave."

Annie could see that the girls were torn. The fun of playing sympathetic listeners had quickly worn off, but the two girls hated to miss anything. Grace understood their hesitation. "Did you see the new hats at the milliner's?" she asked. "There were several pretty ones in the window this morning." She smiled blandly at the girls who immediately began to put on their cloaks and hoods.

When Letty and Diana had gone, Grace said to Virginia, "Go to your father and find out what medicines Mistress Hallan should take with her. Tell him to charge it to my father's account and bring those things with you." When Virginia looked uncertain, Grace gave her a gentle push. "Tell him to send everything that would be helpful."

Now it was just Kate, Annie, and Grace. Mistress Hallan seemed willing to let the girls take charge. Grace looked at Kate and said, "Have you ever packed a trunk?"

AN EMERGENCY

Nodding, Kate said, "I help my mama do for Mrs. Wythe all the time."

"Then go and pack a trunk for Mistress Hallan. Her girl is not very helpful, but if you take her with you, she can show you where to find things." Kate didn't hesitate. Within seconds she had taken the servant girl in hand and begun the job of packing.

Now Grace looked at Annie, and the girl felt ashamed that there was nothing practical she could do to help. But Grace had other ideas. "Can you run?" she asked her.

With embarrassment, Annie said yes. She knew young ladies didn't run.

"Good," Grace answered, obviously pleased. "Would you be willing to run to my house and get a carriage. Mistress Hallan's family lives about fifteen miles from here, and there is no reason for her to rent a coach. My family can spare one. I sent my carriage back home, but if you wouldn't mind going after it, I could finish up here and we would be ready by the time you came back."

Annie hesitated only a minute, but it was long enough for Grace to blush. "I would go myself, you understand. But with these silly hoops, I am helpless. I just saw that you were more sensibly dressed."

A grin flashed across Annie's face. "Of course I can run," she said, immediately wanting to be out the door. It seemed even more fun because there was something slightly improper about it that appealed to Annie's sense of mischief. "Who would ever connect the governor's daughter to a girl running down the street?" she laughed. "Shouldn't you write me a note?"

"Of course," Grace answered, as she took a sheaf of paper from Mistress Hallan's desk and dipped a quill into the inkstand. She scrawled a note, blotted it carefully, put it in an envelope, and sealed it with a drop of wax. "Just hand this to the doorman. He will know what to do."

Annie had opened the door and was down the stairs before she realized she did not know where Grace lived.

"When you get past the capitol, turn to your right. You will see the Hall in the distance past York Street. If you have trouble, just ask at the gunsmith's. He will help you."

Once out the door, Annie began to run. Instead of going down busy Duke of Gloucester Street, she cut through the gated backyards until she reached Francis Street. She ran past the little houses that lined the street and past the dying vegetable gardens. Several cows grazed in a common area, and the sheep seemed to graze anywhere there was grass. When she developed a stitch in her side she slowed down to a walk, ignoring the curious glances of the townsfolk who were going about their business. Finally, on the right, she saw the gunsmith. She knocked timidly at the door of the house that was connected to his shop. A white-haired woman answered and pointed the way to the Hall.

Annie walked up the long tree-lined driveway to Grace's house, aware that her cheeks was red and her hair had tumbled out of its cap. She paused near a tree, taking a minute to wipe her face on a petticoat and to smooth her hair. Footsteps on the oystershell drive gave her a start, and she looked up to see a tall, thin man, about Patsy's age, who looked at her with curious gray eyes. "Good morning," he said in a deep voice. "May I give you some assistance?"

Straightening up, Annie curtsied, feeling the heat rise in her cheeks. "Excuse me," she stuttered. "I am Annie Henry. Grace sent me to get a carriage for Mistress Hallan who must go home because of the pox." The words tumbled out so fast that they were hardly understandable to the man.

With a small bow, he introduced himself. "I am Spencer Roane, a cousin of the fair Grace, and confused about your errand. But I am sure that the ever-organized Grace has sent along a message explaining it." He looked expectantly at Annie, who only then remembered the letter she carried in her hand. She held it out to him, and he tore the seal and read it quickly.

"Let us go back to the carriage house and see what is suitable for this trip." He held his arm out to her, and Annie placed her fingers on his elbow as she had seen fashionable ladies do. She almost stumbled over her feet, as she sought to keep up with his long stride. Between Mr. Roane and the groom, a decision was soon made about which carriage and horses to send. Then Grace's cousin, as though realizing he'd had a dreadful lapse in manners, said, "I am so sorry. I should have offered you some refreshment. Would cider do?"

Annie nodded, unable to utter even the most simple phrases. Never had she felt so tongue-tied as in the presence of this gentleman. He stared at her intently. "Didn't I meet you with your father coming into Williamsburg?" he asked.

All of a sudden Annie recalled the young man who had fixed their wheel and escorted them from Richmond. She blushed as she pictured how disheveled she must appear. "I didn't recognize you," she said apologetically.

"Nor I you," he added with a laugh. They stood there awkwardly for a minute before he, sensing her discomfort, abruptly excused himself and walked toward the house.

Soon the carriage was ready, and the driver helped Annie inside. She laid back against the soft leather seat and thought that this carriage, with its polished wood and gold appointments, was not the carriage of an everyday lawyer. Certainly Patrick Henry had never owned anything like this.

At Mistress Hallan's they found the school teacher out front with her trunk, waiting on the brick sidewalk, Grace at her side. As the driver helped the teacher into the carriage, Annie took her place next to her classmate. The teacher waved at the girls as the two black horses, responding to the urging of the driver, set off down the street.

WILLIAMSBURG

THE SUN WAS OUT, THE AIR WAS CRISP AND CLEAN-smelling. And best of all, there was a whole day ahead with no school. "What do we do now?" Annie asked with anticipation as she watched the carriage disappear down the street.

Grace grabbed her hand. "Come with me and I will show you Williamsburg."

Hand in hand, the girls walked toward the main street, which was filled with carriages and wagons.

"I've never seen so many wagons here," Annie said.

"Market Days are coming next week," Grace answered. "These folks are setting up early to get the best spots."

Indeed, the streets were full of people and wagons. Small boys ran in and out between the carts, causing more than one driver to raise his whip as though to strike the grinning children.

Next to the courthouse there were many bewigged

gentlemen. "Court is in session," Grace whispered. "They'll be holding trials for all the thieves and scoundrels." As the girls passed the courthouse, Annie saw a man with his arms and head in the stocks. She turned away in embarrassment as a small boy threw a hickory nut that hit the man on the head.

"What's he done?" Annie whispered.

"Probably public drunkeness," Grace answered.

"Look," Grace said, pointing to a broadside that had been posted on a wall. "There will be horse racing and a play called *The Tragedy of Othello.*"

"Does your family allow you to go?" Annie asked, feeling every bit the country girl she was.

"Of course. Everybody goes. The town will be so full, there won't be a room in a tavern that's not taken. Papa says that men even share a bed because it is so crowded. Relatives come to visit us from all over. Why, I remember two fairs ago; we had twenty-five extra people staying at our house, and they stayed for weeks even though the fair lasts only three days."

"I met one of your relatives," Annie said shyly.

"And who might that have been?" Grace asked.

"He said his name was Mr. Roane. . . ." Annie couldn't figure out why the tall stranger had made her so tongue-tied.

"Oh, cousin Spencer. He's awful handsome, don't you think?" Grace glanced at Annie mischievously. "They say he's one of Virginia's most eligible bachelors."

By this time Annie knew she was blushing terribly. In order to change the subject, she pointed to another broad-side. "Look at this," she said, and then began reading the notice:

THURSDAY NEXT, THERE IS TO BE A TRYAL OF SKILL, WITH BACK SWORDS, PERFORMED ON THE PUBLICK STAGE BY TWO GLADIATORS, ONE AN ENGLISHMAN. THEY BOTH DESIRE SHARP SWORDS, A CLEAR STAGE, AND NO FAVOUR.

"What does that mean?" she asked her friend.

"Oh, it will be sword fighting. . . very dramatic, I should think. And there will be crowds of people about the stage, and the men will be wagering. . . ."

"But might someone get hurt?"

"I don't think so. I rather think it is a show and the men just pretend to go at each other with swords and dag-gers. But I am only guessing. Mother says the outdoor sports aren't for children or ladies. She won't let me go to the cockfights or the bearbaiting either; though I've heard it is awfully bloody, so I don't really want to see it anyway."

They'd been so busy talking that Annie hadn't realized they had come upon the Raleigh Tavern. A crowd had gath-ered in front of the white clapboard building, and Annie and Grace paused to see what was happening. From a small platform, a man held up a clock. Around him, men dressed in wigs stood alongside laborers who wore their own hair pulled back and tied behind their necks, raising their hands and nodding their heads in a kind of silent ritual. Only the man with the clock spoke, and his was a singsong.

"An auction," Grace cried. "I do love auctions. Watch how they raise their bids."

Annie watched and soon she began to understand the meaning of the jerky hand motions. Between items, there was much teasing and joking back and forth, and the crowd of men did not seem to be taking the bidding all that seriously

"Look," said Grace, "isn't this pitiful? Parson Field's widow is selling all her things so that she can go out West. I wouldn't go West even if you paid me. Can you imagine living in those horrid conditions? With wild Indians about." As Grace spoke, she rifled through the boxes, tsk-tsking at the odd assortment of goods being sold. "Who would buy some of these things?" she asked.

Annie shrugged, ready to move on. The auctioneer had just sold a table and lamp, and was moving toward the box of knicknacks. He looked up at the girls, an annoyed expression on his face. "This is hardly the place for you," he said. "Why don't you go on about your business and let me get back to mine?"

Two little red circles flamed in Grace's cheeks. "I'll have you know that you are speaking to the governor's daughter," she said haughtily, pointing at Annie. The man had come so close that the girls could smell the tobacco on his breath and see the grease stains on his shirt front.

He stared at them boldly. Then he took a soiled hander-chief from his pocket and wiped his nose, all the time keeping his smallish eyes on her.

The man frightened Annie. If it had been her choice, she would have run away, but Grace grabbed her arm and held it so tight that she couldn't move.

"I don't think you want to be rude to the governor's daughter, do you?" Grace persisted. "After all, he could shut down your little auction business if he wanted to."

The man looked furious. The veins in his neck pulsed with anger. For a minute, Annie thought he was going to curse at Grace. But then he seemed to think better of it. He trained his piggy eyes on Annie, who flinched under his gaze. A small smile stole across his face.

"I didn't mean to be rude to our nobility," he said smoothly. "Let me make amends to you," he continued, holding out to her a little box. When she hesitated, he pushed it on her. "Now you take this little gift as a present from me, and we will be friends, won't we?"

Annie began to protest, but Grace pinched her arm so hard it brought tears to her eyes. She felt her fingers close over the box. Immediately Grace began tugging at the girl's arm, pulling her away from the auction scene. When they reached a clearing, Annie turned on her friend.

"How could you do that?" she demanded. "My father will be furious."

"Oh fiddlesticks," Grace answered. "That's how things work here. People are glad to do favors for you, and you should let them do it. All the other governors did that. The people expect it. Open the box, anyway. What did he give you?"

Annie shoved the box at her friend. "You take it, if it means so much to you," she said. But Grace would have none of it.

"I didn't figure you to be such a prude," Grace said with disgust. "I should have come with Diana and Letitia, though they are frightfully boring."

Annie didn't like to be thought of as a prude. Besides, she was curious. What had the man given her? She lifted the hinged top of the small wooden box, and nestled there was a beautiful tortoiseshell hair comb.

"It's beautiful," Grace said with surprise. "I thought he'd given you some awful glass beads, but this is a lovely comb. Take off your cap and put it on," she demanded.

It wasn't the first time that day that Annie had felt a little like a marionnette puppet being jerked around by her demanding friend. Nonetheless, she pulled off her cotton cap and slipped the comb into her thick brown curls. Annie knew from Grace's admiring expression that the comb looked good on her, but she asked the question anyway, "How does it look?"

"It looks wonderful," Grace said. "It will look even nicer when you get some proper clothes."

Annie didn't let Grace's insult bother her. She felt enlivened by their escapade. It could be fun being the governor's daughter, she thought. Her father had told her she would enjoy it. Maybe this is what he meant.

For the next hour the girls amused themselves by promenading up and down the sidewalks in front of the shops, giggling behind their fans when they saw any of the young men staring. Annie found that she enjoyed the stares, and she wondered why she had fussed so about getting older. Maybe Patsy had been right all the time. It was only after a while, though, that Annie remembered to ask Grace a question that had bothered her all morning.

"Why did you change Kate's ink?"

The other girl said, "It gets so dull at Mistress Hallan's. I thought it would be something different. But I never thought Kate would be so upset. She's usually so. . . quiet."

"It seems so unfair that Mistress Hallan blames her for everything. Why didn't you confess?"

Grace gave Annie a quizzical look. "If you had played a prank, would you confess if it might bring shame to your father? Would you really want to disgrace him and make his job harder?"

Thinking of it that way, Annie was no longer certain. She shrugged.

"Well, that's how I felt. Kate doesn't have a reputation. She's a servant. But my father is a prominent attorney. You heard Mistress Hallan. I can't be the one to dishonor him."

"But why not be nice?" Annie couldn't help but ask.

"Now you're acting like a prude again. Don't you ever want to do something fun if it doesn't hurt anyone?"

Grace's voice rose, and Annie saw several people turn to look at them. She didn't want to fight. Besides, Grace was fun. She was bold, and it was certainly good to have a friend in Williamsburg, especially one with so much style, so she changed the subject.

"I'm hungry. Is there someplace we could eat?"

"We can eat in the dining room at the Raleigh but not in the tavern," Grace answered. The girls headed across the street, dodging the carriages. They took their seats near a table where two men, dressed in striped silk breeches and long velvet coats, sat. On their heads they wore stacked and curled wigs in an outrageous style.

Annie couldn't help but stare since she had never seen a man dressed in that fashion. But Grace merely giggled. "Aren't they handsome?" she said. "Father says there are many macaronis in London, for the people are much more stylish there."

As the girls ate, the dandies rose from their chair and made elaborate bows toward the two young ladies, which made Annie blush and caused even Grace to giggle.

"I think it would be excellent to live in London," Grace said later. "Just imagine the fine life we would have."

"But I thought you were a patriot?" Annie said with surprise.

"Oh, we all are patriots," Grace said dryly. "The patriots are winning, and Father says it is best to be on the winning side. But I think the British soldiers look very handsome in their red coats."

Annie wasn't sure whether her friend was serious or not, so she laughed. They each ate a bowl of sorbet and then left the Raleigh. They admired hats in the milliner's window. Annie saw in the silversmith shop a belt buckle that she felt sure her father would like. In the barber shop they saw a man with a long cone over his nose and mouth. Behind him, the barber (who doubled as the surgeon) sprinkled powder over the man's head until the air was full of fine white dust. With the help of the tube, the man was able to breathe until the dust settled. Finally, the man stood up, removed the cloth that had protected his shoulders from the dust, and glanced admiringly in a mirror at his newly powdered wig. Annie gasped when he turned around. It was her father.

She turned her head abruptly, not wanting to meet him on the street. "I need to go home now," she said to Grace. "I don't want to worry my father."

"He won't be missing you yet, will he?" she asked.

"I don't know. But I want to get home."

"All right. But at least walk me to Mistress Hallan's. That's where my carriage is coming to pick me up."

By the time they reached the market square, behind the courthouse, there were twice as many wagons as before. And already the smell of roasting meats and the call of cheery vendors had begun filling the air.

Annie gazed wistfully at several country boys in their worn breeches, wrestling in a clearing. Though dust-covered and shabby, the boys brought back to Annie memories of her brothers. Despite her best efforts, her eyes began watering, but she was determined not to let her friend see her cry.

"Just a bit of homesickness," she said, when she saw that Grace had seen her wipe away a tear. "I guess I miss the boys."

"You have brothers?" Grace asked.

"Oh, yes," Annie said, but for some reason she was reluctant to tell Grace about them.

"How could those country boys remind you of your brothers?" Grace asked.

Annie shrugged and said, "You know, boys . . ."

Annie was glad when they reached Mistress Hallan's and saw Grace's carriage, which had come back to fetch her home. She waved and said, "Thank you for the tour of Williamsburg."

"It was fun," Grace said. "And rewarding for you."

At those words, Annie's hands flew to her head, where she could feel the comb under her cap. She couldn't keep the grin off her face.

"Perhaps we can go to the fair together," Grace said.

"I'd like that," Annie replied with a wave as Grace's carriage rolled down the road.

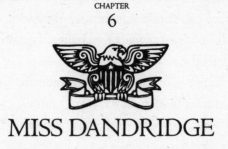

MISS DANDRIDGE

BY THE TIME ANNIE ARRIVED AT THE PALACE, HER father was already there. He greeted her enthusiastically and said, "I feel stronger today than I have in a long time. Come, sit with me outside. Soon it will be winter and too cold."

When they had taken seats out in a sunny spot on the lawn, Patrick Henry asked about Annie's day. Glad for his undivided attention, she told him about Mistress Hallan and then about her tour of Williamsburg.

But Annie didn't mention the auction, sensing that her father wouldn't approve. She nervously fiddled with the comb, which she could feel under her cap, and she was glad that she didn't have to explain to him how she had gotten it.

Annie wasn't use to hiding secrets, and having one made her eager to go inside. She rose to go back to the house, but her father held her arm. "There is something I want to tell you," he said, turning his face away from hers.

His expression was not one that Annie had seen before. He looked younger, in a way, and a secret smile played about the corners of his mouth. When he caught Annie staring at him, a slow blush colored his cheeks.

"We'll be having a guest for dinner," he said abruptly. "You should dress for the occasion."

"But I don't have any dresses," Annie said. "I only have the clothes I brought with me from home."

"And what is wrong with those clothes?" her father asked.

"There isn't anything wrong with them," his daughter said shyly. "But none of the girls at school dress like this. . . except for the girl who works for Mrs. Wythe."

Her father was quiet for a minute. Clearly, this was news to him. "Well, it isn't fitting for my daughter to be improperly dressed," he said. "But what do we do about it?"

Annie shrugged. She didn't know anything about dressmakers. That had been Patsy's job.

Patrick Henry smiled suddenly. "Miss Dandridge, she's the guest who is coming to dinner, she'll know what to do about it. We'll leave your clothes in her hands."

With a frown, Annie considered her father's words. She didn't want to depend on the lady she had seen with her father. On the other hand, the woman would know about clothes. Feeling confused, the girl excused herself and ran inside.

Later, when Annie entered the dining room, she saw a flower-decorated table that was laden with food. But

Annie's eyes did not linger on the table, because behind it stood a pretty young woman, whose hair was piled high and dressed with pearls. She was laughing playfully with Annie's father, who stood next to her, until both of them became aware of the young girl's presence.

Abruptly, they broke off their conversation, and Patrick Henry intoduced his companion, "Miss Dandridge, I would like you to meet my daughter, Annie. Annie, Miss Dandridge."

Annie could feel their eyes upon her as she curtsied. She was glad when it was time to sit and eat. Despite the best efforts of her father and his friend, dinner was an uncomfortable affair, filled with awkward pauses. Every time Miss Dandridge tried to engage her in conversation, Annie couldn't think of the simplest thing to talk about.

Finally, Patrick Henry cleared his throat. Annie held her breath, fearing that he was making some kind of announcement. But instead, he said in a loud voice, "Dorothea, we must do something about Annie's clothes. She tells me she is not dressed properly for Williamsburg, and I have been negligent. Well, I want to remedy the situation, but neither I nor Annie know anything about it. Will you take pity on this poor child and see that she is outfitted correctly?"

While this little speech was going on, Annie thought that she would die. Especially when her father made her stand and turn so that Miss Dandridge could see the problems with her current dress. How could he be so clumsy? she thought. She refused to smile or even look at her father's friend.

Finally, when she thought the humiliation would never end, she heard Miss Dandridge say in a sweet voice, "Why don't we have a little music. Patrick, won't you play for us?"

He excused himself and went to the fortepiano, which sat in the corner. As soon as he left the table, Miss Dandridge reached out a hand to sullen Annie. "Your father meant no harm, child. He didn't mean to embarrass you, nor did I. If you are willing, though, I would love to help you pick out some fabrics for some new clothes. I have a marvelous dressmaker, and it would be my pleasure."

It was hard to be angry at Miss Dandridge. After all, it wasn't this woman's fault. With a shy smile, Annie agreed.

"Good. I'll come for you tomorrow morning," the woman said. "Now let us go over to the piano and sing."

☆

The next morning Miss Dandridge and Annie rode in a carriage to the dressmaker's house, which was behind a milliner's. Miss Dandridge sent the carriage away with orders to come back in an hour. As Annie hung back, looking admiringly at some of the feathered hats in the milliner's window, Miss Dandridge went ahead and knocked on the dressmaker's door.

Once inside, they were in a room full of fabric. Some was silk, obviously imported years before, and now being sold for very high prices. But there were also pretty cottons, damasks, and satins, some from America, but mostly from France. Miss Dandridge looked around and began pulling out bolts of fabric. "Do you like this? Do you like that?" she asked, and Annie, who felt too timid to answer, merely shrugged. The dressmaker smiled at the confusion, and when there were eight bolts on the table, she said, "I think that is plenty to choose from."

"So it is," Miss Dandridge said, satisfied that she had done her job. "Now this little girl would like several dresses, three I think, suitable for school. And one dress for parties."

"Four dresses," Annie gasped. "What will Father say?"

"Your father will be glad," Miss Dandridge answered.

"Have you ever worn hoops?" the dressmaker asked. Annie shook her head.

"Well then, we must start you with a pair of pocket hoops. She pulled a contraption off a shelf. "This is a pocket hoop farthingale," she said as she buckled the leather strap around Annie's waist. From the leather belt hung four metal braces, and from the braces were three half circle hoops on each side. The top hoop was smallest, the next a little bigger, and the bottom hoop was the largest. These hoops were strung together, and if a woman needed to fit through a small door, the hoops on one side could collapse.

Annie surveyed herself with the hoops and sighed. "Will I be able to run?" she asked.

"I'm sorry," the dressmaker said. "Once you are in hoops, your running days are over."

Before Annie could change her mind, Miss Dandridge said, "Look at the bright side of things. You'll soon be old enough for courting and marriage, and you won't even want to run."

Annie rolled her eyes, but she was too polite to argue with the older woman. Next, the dressmaker removed a petticoat from a shelf. "You will need new petticoats to go over these hoops," she said. The petticoat was heavier than anything Annie had ever worn. It was made of two layers of fabric quilted together, with wool batting in between.

Miss Dandridge laughed when she saw the effect that the petticoat and the hoops made. The slender child had grown a foot wider on either side, as the hoops held the skirt out at the hips. But since the hoops didn't extend in the front or the back, Annie looked perfectly flat.

"I look like a loaf of bread that has been run over by a wagon," she said. "Flat from front to back, and bulging at the sides."

The dressmaker tsked and continued her measuring and pinning until, at last, she announced that she was finished. "Now choose your fabrics," she said through a mouthful of pins.

Annie looked at the pretty cottons that sat before her and finally settled on three, with the help of Miss Dandridge. Choosing fabric for a party dress was more difficult, but she finally settled on a dark green satin.

"Could you have one of these made up right away?"

Miss Dandridge asked. "I know Miss Henry would like to have a new dress for market days."

The dressmaker nodded. "I will begin it today. It is not too fancy. I can have it done early next week, before the fair begins."

Miss Dandridge nodded with satisfaction. "Send it by the governor's house just as soon as it is ready, please."

☆

Annie was quiet on the ride back to the Palace. "That wasn't so hard, was it?" the older woman said.

"The dresses will be lovely," Annie admitted. "But will I like wearing them?"

"You really don't have much choice, my dear. The fate of all young girls is to become young women. That is the way God planned it. The hard part is becoming a young woman of good character—a godly young woman. That doesn't happen naturally."

"Did you ever wonder why people act so funny?" Annie asked.

"What do you mean?"

The girl shook her head. She wasn't sure what she meant, but she surely felt confused.

The carriage stopped at the governor's house, and Annie stepped down. She smiled shyly at her father's friend. "Thank you for helping me," she said.

"I loved doing it," the older woman replied. "I hope you'll let me be a friend."

CHAPTER

7

THE FAIR

TIME SEEMED TO CRAWL AS ANNIE LOOKED FORWARD to market days. Finally the first day arrived, and the poor girl woke with a throbbing headache. She cracked her eyes opened and winced as the sun poured through her bedroom window. With a groan, she pulled the covers up over her head and tried to go back to sleep. But the headache, which had been a mild irritation as she slept, now strengthened, and Annie worried for a minute that she was sick again as she had been about a year earlier with the fever.

She heard a knock and the door opened. Then came the sound of the maid's soft footsteps across the floor. Still, Annie didn't budge. It wasn't until the maid said, "I've brought you some hot tea and a letter from home" that she threw back the coverlet and sat up abruptly in her bed. The maid saw her wince and immediately asked, "Are you ill, Miss Annie? Should I get your father?"

"No. I just have a terrible headache, and the light from

the window is awfully bright," she said, trying to keep the whining out of her voice.

The maid pulled the drapes closed, and Annie felt better almost at once. Taking a quick sip of the hot herb tea, she turned the letter over in her hand, but she didn't open it. Instead, she waited impatiently for the maid to pick up some clothes off the floor and smooth the covers because she did not want to open the letter while anyone was there. It was hers, and she wanted to read it alone.

Finally, when the girl thought she could bear it no longer, the maid left. She quickly slipped the blade of the letter opener under the sealing wax and broke the seal. The letter smelled of lavender and brought back memories of sachets made from the dried blossoms that grew in the herb garden at home. It was funny the things she remembered.

Dear Sister,

We have been poorly at Scotchtown. Such a season of illness I do not remember, but God has spared our lives though many are still weak from the effects of this bout of flu.

The rain continues, day after day, and I feared the crops might be lost in the fields, but husband John has managed to bring them in, and I think we will do well.

Annie looked up from the letter and thought about the hard work of bringing in the wheat. It had been only two years since she had helped save the crop from fire.

Your brothers chomp at the bit to be off with General Washington's army, but John Fontaine has reminded them how the army in the north depends on food from our Virginia farms. We have been divided into sections, each with the duty to send a portion of our bounty to the army. John Fontaine has worked hard to gather meat as well as corn and wheat to send up north. We have tried to cut back on our own needs so that we have more to send.

As Annie sat on her canopied bed, she felt a twinge of guilt. Never had she lived so easily as during these weeks at the Governor's Palace, and yet the family at Scotchtown was sacrificing for the army. She turned back to the letter.

Baby grows, and with all the sickness about, he has worn me out. I worried about his taking ill, and now I find I have little energy to manage. And nurse has had her hands full with Elizabeth and Edward. But I must not complain.

The Thackers are well and ask about you. In fact, Andrew and his father are going to market in Williamsburg. Perhaps you will see them. We miss you. Though I was often exasperated by your behavior, I find that our home would be happier if I could hear your laughter and the sound of running feet. Keep Father from getting sick, and remember how much we love you.

Your loving sister,
Patsy

Annie laid the letter aside and brushed away the tears that wet her cheeks. For a fleeting moment she wanted nothing more than to rush back to Scotchtown and see the familiar faces. But then she thought of her father, still weak from his own illness, trying to do the hard work of governor. "I'm needed more here," she said aloud.

There was another knock on the door, and once again the maid entered. This time she carried a tray loaded with food and a bottle of some sort of medicine "guaranteed to take away the headache," she promised.

Annie forced herself to eat some of the hominy. Under the maid's watchful eye, she swallowed a spoonful of the bitter remedy, washing the foul taste down with another sip of tea.

"There is a card for you, miss," the maid said hesitantly.

Annie reached for the engraved card that was on her tray. Printed on heavy ivory paper was Grace's name. On the back, in her friend's neat handwriting, was a note.

Come to the fair with me today. Could you meet me at the church yard at noon? Send a response with my driver.

Annie considered. Did she feel well enough to go? Carefully, she turned her head from side to side. Her headache seemed to be going away—it no longer hurt when she moved her head. Rising from her bed, she walked over to her desk where she kept her pen and ink. In a careful hand, she wrote that she would be pleased to go and signed her name. After blotting the paper, she handed the letter to her maid with instructions to take it down to the waiting driver.

There was no need to hurry, so Annie rested a little longer. But when the clock chimed eleven o'clock, she rose from her bed. The water in the pitcher on her washstand was already cold, so she splashed it quickly on her hands and face. Then she looked in the wardrobe. Only yesterday a package had arrived with one of her new dresses, the hoops, and petticoats. Annie had carried the clumsy bundle upstairs without anyone seeing it. Now, she thought, I will wear my new dress.

When the maid returned, Annie asked her to help. Together they strapped on the hoops. Then Annie pulled on the heavy petticoat. Finally, with the maid's help, she struggled into the tightly corseted gown the dressmaker had sewn. It had narrow sleeves, with a band of lace at the bottom. There was lace around the collar. The skirt was gathered so that the pretty petticoat showed underneath. She moved this way and that in front of the mirror, admiring the way the hoops made her skirts stick out on the sides. The whole costume weighed at least fifteen pounds, Annie thought. "I look all grown-up," she said to herself.

Although Miss Dandridge had given Annie a pair of tiny leather shoes, they didn't look as though they could stand up to walking, so Annie put on a pair of sturdy boots. No one would see them under the dress, she thought.

By the time she left the Palace it was close to noon. She

tried to hurry, but she had to squeeze through sidewalks full of people. There were fancy people and tradespeople in plain dress, farmers, and macaronis. The market itself was on the green near the courthouse, but the Palace green was also crowded with carriages and horses. From a distance, she could hear faint music coming from some sort of high-pitched instrument. It was nearly drowned out by a multitude of voices. Twice the girl was nearly run over by a runaway horse that galloped back and forth across the street.

Annie could hardly keep her eyes still. There was a juggler on one side and a man with two monkeys on his shoulder on the other. Up ahead she saw a roped-off area where two boys wrestled, while the crowd cheered them on. Just when she wondered if she should return home, she saw Grace alight from a carriage. Ignoring the crowds around her, Annie pushed forward to meet her friend. In her haste, and because she was not accustomed to her hoops, she bowled over a small child without realizing it. His cries caught her attention, and she stopped and picked him up, ignoring the teasing of an older boy who said, "Watch where you're going, miss."

Grace was tapping her foot impatiently while she waited for Annie. When she saw her friend, she grabbed Annie's arm and said, "You look marvelous. That is a lovely dress. Now come. We don't want to miss a thing."

"Where do we start?" Annie asked.

"Let's go see the sword fighting," Grace answered, a mischievous smile on her face.

"But I thought ladies didn't do that," Annie answered a bit uncomfortably.

"Oh, pshaw," Grace answered. "That was a rule set by the royal governor. But we don't have a royal governor anymore. We can make our own rules."

Annie thought about that. It seemed to make some sense, so she followed behind her friend.

They walked across the green, away from the street. The farther they went, the fewer girls and ladies Annie saw. Up ahead, a small stage had been erected, and upon it, two men dressed only in breeches and loose, white shirts held their swords aloft. A signal was given and the men began their dance, lunging at one another with their swords as the crowd around them cheered. Spectators were betting on the outcome of the fight, and men in the corners had their hands full of money.

It was dramatic, and Annie found herself moving closer to the stage as she watched it. She blushed when she heard the cursing going on, and several times she thought someone said something crude to her as she walked past. But the girl was so enthralled by the fight that she lost track of time and place.

Finally, the fight was finished when one of the swordsmen managed to pin the other against the rope at the side of the stage. Annie felt Grace tug at her arm. She turned to go but found that it wasn't Grace who was tugging at her. It was a foul-smelling man carrying a large jug of ale who was pulling her arm. His fat, red face was uncomfortably close to Annie's.

"Ah, the governor's daughter," he sneered. "You want to come and have a friendly drink with me?" he added, leering.

Annie recognized the drunken man as the auctioneer. She tried to pull away, but he had his dirty hands on her dress and she was afraid it would tear. She looked around desperately for Grace but couldn't see her anywhere.

"Let go," she hissed at the man, but he held her arm more tightly with his dirt-covered hand.

"I thought we were going to be friends," he whispered, his breath hot against her cheek. Annie was about ready to scream when she felt a hand on her other arm. "I've been looking for you, young lady," said a tall man on her left. "Cousin Grace asked me to find you, and so I have."

Annie had never felt so relieved in her life. It was Spencer Roane, Grace's cousin, who stood protectively next to her. He looked at the red-faced man and said firmly, "I'll take my little friend with me." Annie thought for a minute there would be a fight, but the man let go, muttering insults all the time.

Her cheeks burned as she heard the things the auctioneer said about her and realized that Mr. Roane had heard them too. Annie could feel the hot tears stream down her cheeks. She tried desperately to blink them away. Blindly, she followed her rescuer, who held her tightly by the hand as they pushed their way through the crowd. Eventually they stopped, and Annie felt his arms on her shoulders. "You girls were foolish to go there," he said. Annie looked up and saw that Grace was standing, white-faced, next to her. Her normally confident manner had evaporated. She nodded wordlessly as Spencer Roane continued scolding them. Annie felt her headache begin pounding again.

Spencer sighed. "You girls look as though you could use a refreshment. Come, I will buy you a cider."

They followed meekly behind as he led them to an outdoor stall where fresh cider and doughnuts were being served. Even after Mr. Roane left, leaving behind a strict warning that they should stay near the street, Annie and Grace said little.

"I didn't mean to lose you in the crowd," Grace said sheepishly. "I'm so sorry. I'm glad Spencer came by at the right time."

"Me too," Annie whispered.

"Do you want to go home?"

Annie thought about it. She had been scared, but there was no reason to be afraid any longer. As long as they stayed near the street and among the vendors, there would be no danger. And her headache seemed better after the cider and doughnut. Annie shook her head: "But let's not get into any more trouble," she said.

Grace grinned. "Let's not."

The rest of the afternoon was full of many strange sights. Vendors of all sorts sold produce and goods they had brought from all over Virginia and the world. Men and women roasted chestnuts over fires, and small pigs turned on spits over others. In the middle of the green, the girls heard laughing and saw many children racing to see. They found themselves witnessing a soaped pig contest. There, a pig whose tail had been soaped was let loose, and children of all ages chased him around a clearing, trying to grab on to his slippery tail.

The crowd cheered as a mud-covered boy dove at the frightened pig and brought him down. Annie watched for a minute as boy and beast wallowed together in the mire. She only turned away when Grace pulled her in another direction. Then she heard a voice behind her yell, "Annie. . . Annie Henry."

Turning to see who could be calling her name, she came face-to-face with the mud-covered boy from the pig contest. She stared at him for a minute until she spied, through the mud, the smile of her friend from back home, Andrew Thacker.

With a whoop, she ran forward ready to throw her arms around the muddy boy until he said with a laugh, "You'll be an awful sight if you become as muddy as me."

She paused. "Andrew Thacker," she said. "I can't believe I'm seeing you."

"Well, I can't believe I'm seeing you," he said, staring at her fancy dress. Annie blushed as she remembered the scrapes they had been in together. There was an awkward moment and then Annie remembered Grace, who stood behind her waiting to be introduced. "Oh," she said with embarrassment. "Grace, let me introduce Andrew Thacker, a friend from home. . . and Andrew, this is my friend Grace Glendon-Jones."

Andrew removed his cap and bowed, saying, to Annie's astonishment, "Pleased to meet you, miss."

Grace nodded, amusement written on her face. Annie glanced from one friend to the other and grew increasingly uncomfortable, but Andrew rescued the situation. "I have to go now," he said, bowing again. "It was nice to see you, Annie."

Annie watched as he turned and ran through the crowd, wanting to yell out after him but catching herself.

"Interesting friends you have," Grace said slyly. "Not a typical Williamsburg fellow."

Annie began to protest, but that made Grace grin more. Shrugging, she thought, why should she defend Andrew anyway? He had looked ridiculous covered with mud.

She felt her headache returning and was glad when it was time to go home. After gratefully closing her bedroom door, she pulled the drapes on the crowds down below. She removed her dress, which she let slide to the floor, took off the heavy petticoats and hoops, and slid under the covers of her bed.

A knock on the door several hours later woke her. The maid whispered into the darkened room, "Miss Annie, your father is asking to see you. Will you go to him?"

Rubbing the sleep from her eyes, Annie stared for a minute without comprehension. Her body felt heavy, and her legs and arms ached. When she tried to talk, her tongue felt thick and her mouth was dry. The maid slipped a cool hand against her forehead and said, "You're hot. I knew you shouldn't go off to the fair today. I'm going to get you something to make you feel better."

As she pulled the door shut behind her, Annie smiled at the memory of the fair until she remembered Andrew. "What's wrong with me?" she moaned with embarrassment, pulling the coverlet up over her head. "How could I have been so rude to my friend?" Her headache pounded behind her eyes, and her nose was so congested that she could hardly breathe. With every discomfort, Annie felt more and more sorry for herself.

In the midst of her despair, there came a firm rap at her door. The knob turned and Annie heard the door open, but she kept her back toward it, not wanting the maid to see her cry.

"I've brought you something to make you feel better," a gentle voice said. Annie turned to see Miss Dandridge sitting on the side of the bed. When the older woman saw the girl's tear-streaked face, she asked, "What's wrong, my dear? Would it make you feel better to talk about it?"

At first, Annie shook her head.

"Never mind. We don't need to talk now." Miss Dandridge smiled as she smoothed Annie's forehead with a cool cloth. "Just shut your eyes, and we'll see if we can't get that headache to go away." Soon Annie felt herself drift off to sleep.

CHAPTER
8

THE RACE

IT WAS MORNING AGAIN BEFORE ANNIE AWOKE. HER headache was gone, but the maid would not let her out of bed. "Orders of your father and Miss Dandridge," she said.

Several minutes later, Patrick Henry peeked in the door and looked relieved to see Annie sitting up in bed and eating a bit of breakfast.

"You worried me, Daughter," he said, pulling a chair alongside the bed and sitting down in it. "But I can see that Dorothea was correct. She said you were overtired, but she did not think you were ill. She'd like to visit you again if you would enjoy it, and she gave very firm orders that you are not to leave your bed."

As her father spoke, he smiled, clearly enjoying sharing this responsibility with Miss Dandridge. He looked happy. No longer was his skin pale and sickly looking, and his deepset eyes looked less brooding than Annie had seen for a long time. She tried to think how to describe the change that had subtly changed him. Crisper? No, that sounded too much like a piece of toasted bread. Happier? Well, he was clearly that, but the word didn't convey the change in his demeanor. Brighter? Certainly his eyes and smile were brighter, but there was something more. Then she had it. Jaunty! Her father looked absolutely jaunty. There was a spring to his step and a liveliness to all his movements that Annie hadn't seen before. She grinned, and her father, who had been chattering about something, grinned back.

"You seem happy this morning," he said.

"And you also, Father. I haven't seen you looking so jaunty," she said, trying out the new word, "since I was a little girl."

"'Jaunty,' you say? 'Jaunty?'" Patrick Henry roared with laughter, then spoke seriously: "I am happy. And I'm pleased that you noticed. I have news for you."

Annie held her breath and felt her smile evaporate.

"Miss Dandridge and I plan to marry," her father said, not noticing her change in mood. "Isn't that good news?"

"When?" Annie squeaked.

"Early spring," he said. "We want the family to come, and travel is too uncertain in the winter. So as soon as the roads are dry, we will wed."

"Isn't this very sudden, Father?" Annie asked, trying to hide her disappointment. It didn't matter that Miss Dandridge was kind. The girl didn't want to lose her father to another woman.

"I wasn't intending to mention it quite yet," he said, looking at his daughter fondly. "But she told me yes last evening, and I do hate to keep secrets." He looked so pleased with himself that Annie didn't have the heart to show her true feelings.

"It sounds wonderful," she said. Then, slipping back down under the covers, she said, "I'm feeling very tired. Maybe I'll take a little nap."

Her father hopped to his feet. "You rest, Daughter. I must keep some appointments." After brushing her cheek with a kiss, he paused at the door and said, "Andrew and Mr. Thacker will be coming to dinner tonight. I hope you are well enough to join us."

Annie looked surprised. "Will Miss Dandridge be there?" she asked.

"Of course. I'd like her to meet our friends from home."

There was a pause, and Annie fidgeted with the bed-covers. As her father turned to leave, she forced herself to speak. "Won't you be embarrassed?"

"By Miss Dandridge?" Patrick Henry asked. "Not at all, she has lovely manners."

With exasperation, Annie glared at her father. "Not by Miss Dandridge. By the Thackers. They don't seem like Williamsburg people," Annie said, repeating Grace's expression.

Patrick Henry shrugged as though Annie had told a joke. "I guess if the Thackers aren't fit for Williamsburg,

I'm not fit either. We are Hanover County boys, pure and simple. Now you have a quiet day," he said as he left the room.

Annie fell back on her pillows, thinking about her father's words. It was a lot easier for men, she thought. As long as you could shoot a gun and tell a good story, you could belong. But for girls, it was harder. Annie didn't think her father understood at all. Shaking off the gloomy thoughts, she turned her attention to the sounds she could hear from the window.

It was the second day of the fair, and the crowds were as noisy today as they had been yesterday. It was impossible to ignore them. Annie didn't want to have a quiet day, especially upon the orders of Miss Dandridge. She felt fine. She threw on one of her old dresses and went barefoot across the hall to her father's room. There, a large window opened out onto a balcony that overlooked the Palace green. From her perch, she could see the wheelwright working on a carriage and the grooms walking some of the governor's horses.

A crowd was gathering along an oval course, where a group of men and boys were removing their waistcoats and tricornered hats, which they laid in a pile on the ground. Annie watched the men break into groups of five. With much laughing and shoving, one group of five lined up at the starting line and waited. A gun went off and the men burst into motion. The girl watched them race around the course, their ponytails streaming behind them, arms chugging as they stretched toward the finish line. "That looks like such fun," she said wistfully.

When the first group of runners had finished, another lined up at the start and waited its turn to run. She could feel her own heart beating as she longed to be outside running with the others. "Why shouldn't I go?" she asked to herself.

Once the idea had been planted in her mind, Annie bustled about her father's room to see if there were any boys clothes that would fit her. She put on one of the baggy, unbleached cotton tunics that tradesmen wore, and although it was large, it didn't much matter. But breeches would be another problem. Her father's would all be too big. She searched the wardrobe and found nothing. Then she caught sight of the trunk they had brought with them from Scotchtown. It was almost empty, but in the bottom was an old pair of breeches that had belonged to William. It had been packed by mistake in all of the confusion surrounding their departure. Annie pulled them on, fumbling with the buttons. She secured a pair of her father's stockings with garters, slipped her feet into a pair of her own buckle shoes, and admired herself in the mirror.

In all her concern about clothes, Annie had forgotten her hair. "How will I hide it?" she wailed, running over to the window to assure herself that the races were still going on. It looked as though the runners had taken a break while children ran after a flock of sheep that had wandered onto the track.

"I can't wear a hat," she said because she had noticed that all the other runners had removed theirs.

On one table were Patrick Henry's wigs. One had been freshly curled and powdered, but another was in need of grooming. It was dirty, and its ponytail looked straggly. "Father must have worn this in a rainstorm," she muttered, looking at the limp item. "How will it look on me?"

The wig was too large for Annie, but once she tucked her long hair up underneath, it fit fairly tight. She shook her head back and forth and was glad to see that the wig stayed on. Cracking the door, she peeked out and, seeing no one, tiptoed over to the stairwell. Mr. Goodacre was nowhere around. "Now if only I can get downstairs without being seen," she whispered. "It is as good a time as any."

Taking a deep breath, the girl glided silently across the floor and stepped lightly down the stairs. At the bottom, she looked furtively around, then she dashed for the door. Once outside, Annie slowed down. She hoped she looked like any other young boy walking about.

By now the sheep had been herded up and the races were about to resume. Annie watched several more from the sidelines before gathering her courage to go forward. When the last group lined up, she knew it was now or never. She joined them, taking the outermost lane. When the gun sounded, Annie leapt forward, but the men were much faster than she. Although she ran her hardest, she could only overtake one of them. The race ended with

Annie a long way out. But the girl glowed with excitement. It had been fun to run, even if she hadn't won.

Bending over to catch her breath, Annie almost fainted. There, not more than ten feet away, was Spencer Roane. She ducked her head but not before she saw him glancing at her curiously. Keeping her head down, she hurried away, making sure that Mr. Roane did not follow her. After she had slipped into a crowd, Annie turned her attention back to the races. The winners would now compete against each other. Annie picked out Spencer Roane as one of the runners, but there was another who looked familiar. It was Andrew Thacker. Annie would have known his slightly bowlegged walk anywhere. The boy looked nervous. He stood slightly off from the group and glanced every now and then up at the Governor's Palace.

When the gun sounded, Annie jumped. Silently she urged her old friend forward. "Go, Andrew," she whispered and groaned as her friend slipped going around the first curve. But he got up and continued running, gradually overtaking several of the other runners. "Faster, faster," she said a little louder as he rounded the second turn. Soon the runners were close to where Annie stood, and the girl shouted, "Come on, come on," ignoring the strange looks that others gave her. They were all yelling, she thought. Why are they paying attention to me?

Rounding the last curve, there was only one man ahead of Andrew. It was Spencer Roane, Grace's cousin.

"Go, Andrew. You can do it," Annie yelled as loudly as she could. It was only when she heard a whispered comment about girls in boy's clothing that Annie realized she had given herself away with her screaming.

Ducking her face, she pushed into the crowd that was milling about, letting it push and pull her until she was near to the governor's gate. Quickly she slipped through the gate and walked briskly until she was once again in the safety of the Palace. She held her breath, hoping no one would see her as she ran up the back stairs to her room.

She had left her clothes in a jumble on her father's floor. Hurriedly, she pulled off the boy's clothes and pulled on her nightdress, wadding up the breeches and tossing them in the trunk. By this time, her hands were shaking as she realized what she had done and how close she had come to being discovered. As she looked up, she caught a glimpse of herself in the mirror and burst out laughing. For there she was in a simple white gown with a man's white ponytailed wig on her head. She pulled it off and jammed it on the wig stand. There, she thought. Now I look like a frazzled little girl. Taking another deep breath, she opened her father's door and almost ran into Mr. Goodacre, the butler, who stood in the hallway.

"Miss Annie," he said with surprise. "Were you looking for something in your father's room?"

"Just watching from the window," the girl answered

with wide-eyed innocence as she hurried into her own room.

Safely there, Annie found that she was exhausted. She slipped back into bed, where she was soon asleep.

Later that afternoon there was a surprise with Annie's tea. The maid brought up the tray, and hidden among the plates of food was a small box. "A gentleman brought it to you, miss," said the maid with a slight smile.

Annie tried to look indifferent, but she couldn't hide the smile that played around her mouth or lit her eyes. "Are you sure it is for me?" she asked.

"Yes, miss. He said it was for you especially and made me promise to give it to you with your tea."

The maid took her time plumping up pillows and straightening the room, giving a glance every so often at Annie, who was determined not to open the box until the maid had gone. Finally, she left the room, and Annie threw the top off the box. In it, nestled on a piece of cotton wool, were a pair of silver shoe buckles, the prize from the race, and a note. "If pluck and daring were enough to win races, these would be yours," the note read. It was signed with the initials "S.R."

Annie's face burned with embarrassment. Spencer Roane had recognized her. Now Grace would know about her foolish idea to run—and so would her father if Mr. Roane talked about it. The girl held her head in her arms and groaned. "When will I ever learn to think before I act?" she moaned.

THE RACE

☆

At seven o'clock, Annie entered the dining room. She had taken special care in dressing and wore her new dress. The maid had helped curl her hair, which she wore piled on top of her head. The girl was determined to be a lady beyond reproach that evening.

Since her father had invited a large group, tables had been set in the supper room at the back of the house. Someone played the fortepiano while the guests stood in groups talking. As she entered the room, Annie could feel people watching her, and she suspected they were laughing at her. Holding her head high, she walked over to the fortepiano and saw that it was her father who played.

"Daughter," he said, "we have been waiting for you. Come, let us sit down to dinner." He held his arm out to her and led her to a place at one of the tables. Soon all the guests were seated. As the food was served, Annie had time to examine the guests. Next to her father sat Miss Dandridge, and on her other side was Mr. Thacker. It was with surprise that Annie watched the woman talk and laugh with Andrew's father.

Andrew looked less comfortable in his dress-up clothes, and several times Annie caught the boy scowling at her from his place across the table. She didn't know most of the other guests. They were all well-dressed, and she suspected that most were members of the new legislature. The conversation swirled around her as people talked about war and taxes. News had reached Virginia about a British victory in New York. General Washington had lost more than 1,400 troops and had been forced to evacuate Manhattan.

Annie listened with one ear as she thought about her brothers back at Scotchtown. William would soon be eighteen and off to war. Those lost troops could include him, she thought. Even Andrew was getting older and would soon be able to enlist without his father's permission. She could tell by the way he listened to the war talk that he would join General Washington as soon as he was old enough.

When dinner was over, the guests moved into the ballroom to dance. Annie stayed in her chair, not wanting to join the festive group in the other room. Andrew startled her when he said, "Would you go for a walk with me?"

Looking up at her old friend, she shrugged. "Let me get a coat, and I will meet you out back."

THE MAZE

ANNIE HAD CHANGED FROM HER THIN, LEATHER SLIP-pers to a pair of buckle shoes and put on a long, hooded cape. In each hand she carried a lantern, which she brought from the house. Not wanting to go through the ballroom carrying the lanterns and wearing the coat, she left through the side door and circled around the house until she found Andrew shivering in the garden.

"Here," she said, holding out a lantern to him. "It is very dark in the yard."

"Where do you go to get away from this?" the boy asked, waving at the house.

Shrugging, Annie said, "Don't you like the Palace?" He screwed his nose up. "It's so, so. . . showy," he said finally. "It may have suited the royal governors, but it is hardly fitting for the elected governor of the people of Virginia."

Annie immediately took offense. Andrew had a way

of making her angry. "Well, I guess maybe even an elected governor deserves a nice house," she said.

"Oh, you think so," he sneered. "And all these servants and slaves?"

"Why not?" she asked, though she had often thought there were too many servants for such a small household.

"Because we are at war," Andrew said, marching ahead through the yard. "Some people are sacrificing for our freedom. I guess I thought the Henrys would be among them. Besides, Thomas Jefferson's Declaration of Independence said that all men are created equal. How can you keep all these slaves?"

Annie felt herself getting angry. She did not want to argue slavery with Andrew Thacker. "You aren't the only one who has ever sacrificed," she said, quickening her step to keep up with him. "And for your information, Williamsburg suits me. There are real ladies and gentlemen here," she said pointedly. She didn't have to add the next phrase, "unlike in Hanover," because Andrew understood exactly what she was saying. He scowled and she quickened her pace, trying to put some space between them.

"I just don't understand how you could have become so stupid in such a short time," Andrew said to the girl's back. "I always thought you had more sense."

Annie turned and glared at her friend. "Well, that good sense tells me I should go back inside," she said. "Did you ask me to go for a walk so that you could scold me?" Turning again, the girl walked away in a huff.

"Truce," the boy called out apologetically. When Annie turned, he smiled and said in his friendliest voice, "I won't talk anymore about how snobbish and silly the people are in this town." Annie narrowed her eyes and was about to continue the argument when she had an idea.

"Let's go in the maze," she said. "I've never been in it at night. Do you dare?"

The boy nodded, and together the two ran through the garden until they reached the boxwood shrubs that formed the maze.

"The goal is to get to the middle," Annie said. "You go one way; I'll go the other, and we'll see who gets there first."

Before the girl had stopped talking, Andrew set off down his path. The boxwood was thin in places, not nearly as lush as it would be in summer. In the daylight, she could see through the shrubs in spots, but because it was so dark and she had only a lantern by which to see, she had to feel her way along. She held the lantern out before her, letting the candle light the path. With her other hand, she felt the edge of the hedge, feeling for an opening on the side. Up and around the dark path she walked, occasionally seeing the flicker of light from Andrew's lantern or hearing his muttered oath as he tripped over a rock or twig.

"How are you coming?" Annie called out nervously.

"I'm almost there," came the confident reply.

That's not true, the girl thought, but quickened her pace

just the same. She had walked so far without coming to the center clearing that she began to fear that she was lost. *This is silly*, she thought. *I can't get lost in a maze in my own yard.*

"Andrew?" she called out. When he didn't answer, she called again, a little louder. Again there was silence.

Suddenly the girl was afraid. Surrounded by thick darkness, she was overcome by a feeling as though she were caught in a place and could not get out.

"Andrew Thacker, answer me this minute," she yelled, hating the sound of fear she could hear in her own voice. From behind her she heard a deep chuckle, and the girl whirled around. There, standing perfectly still, was Andrew. He had ducked into a path, and Annie had just walked by him without realizing he was there. When she saw his grinning face, she became furious. "How could you do that to me?" she screamed.

Andrew looked surprised. "I didn't mean to scare you that much," he said apologetically.

She was not in the mood to hear an apology. "I hate you, Andrew Thacker," she cried. "You are mean and a big bully, and I hate you." Then she burst into tears.

Andrew looked around him uncomfortably. He had a temper of his own and thought about leaving the angry girl in the maze to teach her a lesson. That was too cruel, he decided. "If there is ever a time to turn the other cheek, now is it," he muttered. Out loud he said, "I'm leaving the maze. If you want me to help you find your way out, come with me."

"And let you get me lost?" she sneered. "I'll get myself out."

"Suit yourself," the boy said. "I trailed a string behind me. Learned it from one of those old stories that Mr. Dabney was so crazy about. Remember the minotaur?"

Annie didn't answer, so he turned and began walking away.

Seeing that he wasn't going to beg her forgiveness, Annie struggled for less than a second about whether to follow him. She hurried to catch up, careful to leave a gap between them. On they walked, saying nothing, until Annie tripped. Her lantern fell to the ground, and the candle snuffed out. Suddenly, it was very dark.

"Andrew," she called. "I've lost my light and twisted my ankle," she cried.

While she waited for the boy to return, she heard rapid breathing from the hedge at her right. Startled, she twisted around to see who was there. "Who's in there?" she demanded with as much authority as she could muster. "I will bring the governor's soldiers to get you," she added when there was still no movement from the bushes. Annie had just uttered those words when she heard Andrew's footsteps and saw the light from his lantern.

He held his hand out to her and pulled her to her feet. She winced as she put weight on the twisted ankle. "Who are you talking to?" he asked.

Annie nodded toward the bushes and whispered, "Someone is in there."

The boy looked at her skeptically. "How do you know that?" he asked.

"Listen. You'll hear breathing." They were quiet, and for a minute there was no sound. Then both of them heard a ragged breath. Andrew said sternly, "Come out from there, now."

The bushes shook, and by the lamplight they watched as first one bare brown foot, then another, appear. The legs were followed in short order by the rest of a young, rag-covered body, topped by a tiny tear-streaked face. The child cowered before Andrew and Annie, keeping her face turned toward the ground.

With her hands on her hips, Annie said, "Get up," as she looked with disgust on the dirty, dark-skinned girl standing before her shivering. Her nubby hair was braided in tight corn rows, and her bare brown legs were gray with dust. Annie's harsh response set the small child shivering.

Andrew interceded. In a gentle voice he said, "Let us go someplace where we can talk. This child is near frozen."

Annie scowled but let herself be led by Andrew, who carried the trembling child. Clumsily they made their way out of the maze. When they had reached the clearing, Andrew paused. Where can we go where we won't be disturbed?" he asked.

"I suppose they are through in the kitchen," Annie muttered. "There will be a fire there, so it will be warm."

The three stumbled through the gardens to the kitchen, which was dark. Hot embers still glowed in the fireplace. Andrew set the girl down on the stone floor and lit several lanterns while motioning Annie to close the door.

The little girl sobbed where Andrew had set her. Annie, who suddenly felt very tired, snapped, "Stop blubbering. It can't be that bad. What reason do you have to carry on so?"

Her harsh words only made the stranger cry louder. Andrew looked impatiently at Annie and said sharply. "That's enough." Then turning his attention to the little girl, he said softly, "What is your name?"

At first she didn't answer, and Annie was about to say perhaps she was deaf when the girl turned to Andrew and whispered, "Deborah."

"How did you come to be in the maze?" Andrew continued, never raising his voice. He had lowered himself to the floor near the little girl and spoke so quietly that Annie, who was standing up, could barely hear.

"I was hiding," she whispered.

"Speak up," Annie said. "What is it? Have you run away? Your master must be looking for you." She ignored Andrew, who said her name several times. Instead, she turned back to the little girl and said, "You'll have to go back, you know. You might as well tell us who your master is, or the guards will force it out of you."

With a desperate voice the child cried out, "Oh missy. Please don't get the guard. Have mercy."

Andrew, in a voice dripping with disgust, said, "Annie, go back to the Palace. I will take care of this."

She turned to argue, but Andrew shook his head. "You've said enough tonight. Now go home."

Like a wounded dog, Annie turned her back on her friend and slipped out the door. Blinded by the tears that streamed down her face, and burning with anger and indignation, she ran to the Palace and slipped in the side door. She could hear voices and music coming from the ballroom, but she turned away from the cheerful sounds and ran up the stairs where she took refuge in her room.

Throwing herself on her bed, she cried and cried. "I hate you, Andrew Thacker," she said, pounding her pillow. Then she remembered her own ugly behavior, and turned her fury on herself. "What has come over me?" she wept. "Why have I become so ugly? Oh God, help me. I am so confused."

CHAPTER
10

AN ERRAND OF MERCY

ANNIE'S TWISTED ANKLE SWELLED HORRIBLY, AND FOR several days she was confined to her room. The doctor said there was no help for it but rest and tight bandages. From her window, she watched as the remaining merchants and farmers took apart their booths and loaded up their wagons. An army of young boys flocked over the green looking for any treasures that might have been left behind.

Once they had gone, the green looked desolate. The catalpa trees had shed their last leaves, which were in sodden clumps along the road. A heavy night rain had washed mud from the fields onto the streets where it sat inches deep along the gutter. It was hard to imagine that Williamsburg could ever look clean again. "It's like my own soul," the girl said to herself. "I've become ugly like this field, and I don't even know how it happened. Is there any hope for me?"

Just then, a wagon rattled down the street toward the Palace. Two men sat on the seat. As it drew nearer, Annie recognized the Thackers. She watched as Mr. Thacker climbed down and entered into a heated discussion with her father, who had been waiting on the steps. Both men stepped aside as a small, blanket-wrapped bundle was loaded on the wagon. She tried to see what was in it but couldn't tell. Finally, the two men shook hands before Mr. Thacker climbed back up and drove off.

As it rolled away, Annie glimpsed two dark brown eyes peering out from under the blanket at the back of the wagon. "They've taken that child," she said in amazement.

It was not until later that day, though, that Annie was able to ask her father about what she had seen. He seemed somber and preoccupied when he came to her room for a visit. But he didn't look surprised when Annie asked, "Where are the Thackers taking that girl?"

Her father didn't answer right away. He studied her face before answering, in a sad voice, "I didn't want to believe the story Andrew told me the other night. . . ."

Though her eyes welled with tears, Annie struggled to hold them back. Lifting her chin, she said in a shaking voice, "I wasn't the one who was rude, Father. It was Andrew. He ordered me back to the house as if I was a child." The injustice of it still burned.

"Yes. Andrew apologized for his rudeness. But I am less concerned with that than I am with your attitude. I have never known you to be cruel or unfeeling."

"Cruel?" she demanded. "I only wanted to let that child know that she couldn't take advantage of the governor."

"Oh, Annie," her father said sadly, rubbing his eyes with the back of his hand. "Did you listen to her story? Did you even stop scolding long enough to listen?"

It was hard for Annie to lie there under her father's disapproving eye. She stared at the blanket rather than meet his gaze, and she felt her heart harden. He didn't understand, she thought. He was always standing up for other people—and not listening to her. He should know that she was only worried about his reputation. After all, Virginia counted on him. When the girl finally looked up, her sulking eyes met her father's sad ones. He shook his head.

"I'm going to tell you her story," he said. "I want you to hear it from me, and then I want you to think about it." Patrick Henry lowered himself into a chair across from her bed. Then he began speaking, his voice so soft that Annie had to strain to hear him.

"Andrew came to me the other night, after settling Deborah—did you know that was her name?—in the kitchen. I found her trembling with cold. Her right cheek was swollen and crusted over with dried blood in a wound that was obviously infected. She had been branded."

Annie interrupted her father. "A brand? Who would brand her?"

"Her master—a man named Mr. Penny from Roanoke."

"I bet she ran away," Annie said. "See, I knew it."

Her father shook his head, closing his eyes as though he was almost too tired to continue. Then his soft voice began again. "Her mother ran away and took Deborah with her. They were caught and given back to the master who branded them—but the mother became sick and died on the trip back to Roanoke. Then, as they were crossing a flooding river, the wagon tipped, and the girl was swept overboard. She grabbed a board that came loose from the wagon. It carried her downstream until she ran into the riverbank. Since then she has been wandering, without food or warm clothing, praying she wouldn't be caught and sent back to the man who put a brand to her face."

Annie shivered, even though her bedroom was warmed by a blazing fire. After her father told the tale, he slumped back in his chair, where he stared past Annie, deep in thought. Annie felt terrible, but her pride and anger wouldn't let her admit it. Finally, her father rose to leave. As he reached the door, he said, "Miss Dandridge has been asking me to let you go with her for several days. I thought it was too cold. But I think the change will do you well. As soon as your leg is better, you will go with her."

For several days Annie puzzled over her father's statement. Where was she going? Why with Miss Dandridge? But he refused to answer any questions. Finally, all the swelling had gone, and Annie was able to walk without pain. That's when he told her, "Today Miss Dandridge will come for you about noon. See that the maid has packed your clothes."

"Yes, Father," Annie said as he pulled the door shut behind him.

After giving the maid instructions about her clothes, Annie felt at loose ends. She decided to go for a walk. The weather had turned cold, but there was no sign of snow. She put on a cape and tucked her hands into a fur muff, then set off down the street, not caring where she went. The wind blew fiercely, biting her cheeks and bringing tears to her eyes. Stopping in front of the print shop to catch her breath, Annie saw a young boy inking type with a leather-covered ball that he dipped into a pan of gooey black ink made of lampblack and varnish. Then he reached up on tiptoes and pulled a long lever, called a devil's tail, which lowered the heavy plate onto the paper. After checking the printing, the boy hung the wet sheet of paper on a drying line.

He glanced up as he worked and caught sight of Annie peering through the window. Screwing his mouth into an awful grimace while crossing his eyes, he stared so intently at her that she blushed and hurried on her way.

The wind had picked up. It howled between the houses, banging a loose shutter on one of them. The streets were nearly empty with only a few brave souls venturing forth. Annie huddled on the sidewalk, pulling her hood more tightly about her face, and burying her cold cheeks in the warm fur of her muff. For a minute, she stood uncertainly on the sidewalk, before turning around and heading back to the Palace. She reached the gate at the same time as a carriage pulled by two gray horses. Miss Dandridge leaned out the window and smiled. "Getting a head start on the cold?"

Barely managing to smile, Annie nodded. "I must get my case and say good-bye to Father. Then I will be out."

Mr. Goodacre carried out a small valise with Annie's clothes. Meanwhile, Annie found her father in the study, still sitting in his chair, brooding. "I'm going, Father," she said, trying to be cheerful.

He looked up, a startled expression on his face. Seeing his daughter before him brought him back to his senses. Rising to his feet, he said, "I hope it will be a good trip for you, Annie." He put his arm around her shoulder and walked her out to the carriage.

"Take good care of her, Dorothea," he said with a smile at Miss Dandridge.

"One day she'll be my daughter, Mr. Henry. I will treat her as one today."

The girl climbed up into the carriage, where Miss Dandridge quickly tucked a heavy fur around her and placed hot bricks at her feet. Even before she was settled, the carriage began moving. By the time Annie looked out the window, her father was almost out of sight. She felt queazy in the stomach and almost shouted for the carriage to stop. Why was she being sent away? And where was she going?

If Miss Dandridge sensed her confusion, she gave no sign of it. Every time Annie looked at the older woman sitting across from her, she had her eyes closed and her head bowed. How could she sleep? the girl wondered.

Annie craned her head out the window and watched each farmhouse pass by. The wind stung, but she didn't care.

Then she became aware that the older woman was watching her. "Where are we going, anyway?" she asked sullenly.

"I have friends in the country who need help. Your father was kind enough to lend you to me."

"What kind of help?" Annie asked, curious about this woman's friends.

"You'll meet them, and God will show you how best to help," Miss Dandridge answered calmly. "It is a long ride. You don't want to freeze."

Annie scowled but pulled back from the window. It wouldn't help if she started out on the wrong foot with this woman her father seemed intent on marrying.

The rest of the trip was quiet. Miss Dandridge was content to doze as Annie stared out the window watching the trees go by. The carriage made good time despite the muddy ground because the road they traveled was well used and maintained. But at a certain point, the carriage turned, leaving firm ground and heading out onto a bumpy, rutted road that was little better than a path. They made their way, lurching and swaying, along the path until, up ahead, Annie caught sight of a small dwelling—little more than a log shack. A mangy looking dog ran out to greet them with ferocious sounding barks, which brought a small boy from the house. He stood on the ramshackle porch, arms drawn close to his shivering body.

As the carriage pulled to a stop, the driver dismounted and helped Miss Dandridge, followed by Annie, out of the coach. It was close to dusk, and the wind, which had subsided, picked up again. It carried a putrid smell, which Annie thought came from a poorly located outhouse. Wrinkling her nose in disgust, the girl turned to Miss Dandridge and was about to comment, but the older woman shook her head and walked briskly toward the ramshackle house, paying no attention to the smell.

With a scowl, the girl lifted her skirts, trying to keep the hem from dragging in the dirt. She quickened her pace to keep up with Miss Dandridge, not wanting to be left outside with the dirty-looking boy who stared at her. He stood in the middle of the doorway, forcing Annie to walk around him, trying to keep her skirts from rubbing up against him. She felt his dark eyes staring at her back as she entered the dimly lit house.

A miserly fire smoldered in the fireplace, giving off little heat. Every time a gust of wind blew outside, the fire flared, fed by the wind that leaked through large gaps between the logs in the walls. Miss Dandridge, ignoring the dirt and cold, put down the satchel she had carried in. She hugged the grimy little boy who had followed them into the house. Annie couldn't help but look to see if the boy's dirty face had left a stain on the older woman's pretty dress.

"Here, Thomas, I've brought you some lovely apple butter and some biscuits to put it on. Why don't you go wash your hands and then you can eat," she said gently as the boy plunged his dirty little hands into the basket of food.

"Yes, ma'am," he said, racing out the door to the well, but not before giving Annie a warning look. She moved away from the basket, thinking to herself, "I don't need his biscuits. He doesn't have to worry about me."

Miss Dandridge went into the bedroom and pulled the room's only chair over to the bed. On it was a woman with a weatherbeaten face. Her arms and neck were covered with scabs. The boy's mother, Annie thought. Miss Dandridge took from her satchel a new shawl, which she wrapped around the other woman's shoulders. "Hello, Mary. How are you this day? Are you eating the food I brought you before? And are you taking your medicine?"

Mary nodded feebly. "The doctor bled me last week," she said in a faint whisper. "Said it would make me better."

Annie shivered thinking of the slimy leeches that were used by doctors to *bleed* patients. But Miss Dandridge didn't even wince. "I heard that your sister left for Bermuda. We were surprised that she would go," Miss Dandridge said.

"Once Mama died, Sissy said there weren't no reason for her to stay. She stayed only long enough to make sure I wouldn't die. She's gone to be with family."

"I guess she feared that if she waited any longer, she wouldn't be able to sail this year. Try not to be bitter. She was fearful of the war."

"I'm not bitter, Miss Dandridge. But it is awful lonesome knowing that there's only me and my boy left here in Virginia."

"You just eat and rest and get your strength back so that you can take care of your boy. You want him to grow up and be a fine man, don't you?"

The sick woman nodded feebly.

"Good. Then I am going to warm some broth for you, and you are going to eat it." Miss Dandridge softened the words with the gentle voice in which they were said.

"Oh, I almost forgot. I brought a helper with me. This is Annie Henry. She was in your sister's class for a while."

Annie had started to smile, but when she heard those words, the smile left her face. Could this really be Mistress Hallan's sister, the one with the pox? Her eyes questioned Miss Dandridge.

"Yes. This is Mary Hallan, sister to your teacher. Sadly, their mother died. But Mary is recovering nicely, and we are here to help for a few days."

Annie looked around the dirty house again. How could Mistress Hallan, so prim and so impressed with position, be related to this person? Annie's face must have reflected her thoughts, because the next thing she knew, Miss Dandridge had pulled her to the side. "I won't have you putting on airs or being rude to my friends," the woman said quietly. "If you cannot help, then you may go outside to the carriage."

Annie blushed red and nodded. The little cabin was

quiet except for the sound of the wind through the cracks. The fire flickered, which seemed to rouse Miss Dandridge from her thoughts. She rose and left the small bedroom. Annie followed her and heard her ask the driver to look for some wood for the fire. That would be a job, Annie thought. There weren't any trees around at all. What a stupid place to build a house.

Just then, she heard a little voice behind her. The boy, Thomas, held a biscuit in his hand.

"I saved this for you," he said. "I wasn't going to give it to you, because I wanted all the biscuits for myself. Then I saw your face, and you looked so angry that I knew I should give you one."

Annie stared at the boy. His lips were smeared with apple butter, and his face was unwashed. He held the biscuit in a hand that, although it had been washed, still was dirty. He smiled shyly at first, until he saw Annie's answering smile. Then a big grin spread across his face.

"Why do you think I'm angry?" she said finally.

"'Cause you look like Aunty, who had a sour face every day she was here," the boy answered bluntly.

"Well, I'm nothing like your aunty," Annie answered, insulted by the comparison.

"Do you want the biscuit?" the boy asked again, looking at it wistfully.

"No. You can have the biscuit," Annie answered. The boy didn't eat, but he continued to look at her expectantly.

"Thank you," she finally said. With that, the boy ate.

CHAPTER

11

ANNIE COMES BACK

WHILE THOMAS FINISHED THE BISCUIT, ANNIE LOOKED around the small room. It certainly needed cleaning. Thomas followed her as she peeked out one of the windows.

"Where does your mama keep a pail?" she asked him.

"On the porch," he said. "Want me to get it?"

"Fill it with water, and we'll clean up this mess," she answered brusquely. As she waited for the little boy to return with the bucket, she looked around. Where could she start? Why had Miss Dandridge brought her to this place? Surely she could have brought a servant. She felt a tug on her skirt and found Thomas standing there with the pail.

"Put it down," she snapped. The little boy's chin quivered, and Annie fought to keep from saying something awful.

"I guess we'll need a broom," she said. "Do you have one?"

"It's on the porch, too. I'll get it," he said, racing out the door and letting it swing shut with a bang.

Annie pushed up her sleeves. She sighed as she looked at her nice new dress with its hoops and lace. It wasn't intended for housework. If Miss Dandridge had told her she was going to be a scullery maid, she could have dressed in her old clothes. For a minute, the girl rebelled. Why should she clean someone else's dirty house? It wasn't her job, and no one could expect the governor's daughter to do it.

The bucket was heavy as Annie lugged it across the plank floor to the corner. There was some lye soap in a cupboard, and Annie scraped some into the water, stirring it with a wooden spoon. She found a clean rag, dunked it into the water, and scrubbed the rough, plank table. It was made of logs that had been smoothed on one side. Bearing down with all her weight, the girl scrubbed and scrubbed until the wood shone. She didn't even hear the boy come back with the broom.

The girl's hands were red from the lye, but she didn't notice. "Thomas, do you know how to sweep?" she asked.

"Yes, miss," he said.

"Then you sweep the dirt out of this house. I'm not doing all the work myself."

The little boy handled the broom awkwardly, but he managed to rid the floor of most of its dirt. "Now I'm going to scrub," she said. But the girl found that it wasn't easy getting on her hands and knees in the clumsy hoop skirt. Putting her hands on her hips, she sighed with frustration. "Turn your back, Thomas," she said.

The boy turned.

She reached under her skirt and undid the buckles that held on her hoops. Slipping them out from under her, the girl felt suddenly free. But she found that her skirt hem dragged on the floor. It was much too long without the hoops to hold it up. "I'm going to have to tie up my hem," she muttered, pulling up the skirt as she spoke. She tied it in several places, letting her petticoat show beneath. Then, plopping down on her hands and knees, she scrubbed.

By the time the floor was finished, Annie's hands were raw. Her back and knees ached, and her skirt was dirty. But the floor had a well-scrubbed look, and the cabin no longer looked so dingy. She stood up and stretched, feeling satisfaction at a job well done.

Thomas, who was standing near the doorway, smiled broadly when he saw how nice the room looked. "It's just like Mama's well again. She used to keep the house neat as a pin," he bragged. "But Aunty wouldn't clean. Said she had a maid at home to do it. And Grandma couldn't, so it just got dirtier and dirtier—I didn't know how to fix it."

Annie nodded, feeling a spark of tenderness toward this grubby little child. "How old are you, Thomas?" she asked.

"I'm seven," he said proudly. "Old enough to be the

man around here, Mama says."

"You are a real help to your mama. I know you are," Annie said. "Come on, there's just one more thing that we need to clean before we are done."

"What is it?" the boy asked, looking around the room.

"It's you, silly," she answered. "Where's your wash tub? I'm going to heat some water and you're going to have a bath."

"A bath," the boy moaned. "I don't need no bath. Mama don't make me take one," he protested.

"But your mama is sick, and I am in charge. And I say you need a bath," the girl said laughing. "Go fetch the water and hang it over the fire. I'll get the tub."

Annie found an iron tub on the porch. It was too cold for Thomas to bathe outside, so she dragged it into the house. Over his protests, she filled it with water that she heated over the fireplace. Only after she agreed to hang a privacy blanket would Thomas undress and climb into the hot water. She waited on her side of the blanket. When it was too quiet in the tub, Annie threatened to come around and make sure the boy was really in the water and using soap. "You scrub behind your ears," she said. "And wash your hair."

While the boy was bathing, Miss Dandridge came out of the bedroom. "Look at this place, Annie. You've done wonders. Where did you learn to clean like this?"

"Last summer when I stayed with a friend at her

father's tavern," Annie said, smiling despite her earlier anger.

"Where is Thomas now?" Miss Dandridge asked.

Annie pointed to the blanket where splashing sounds could be heard. "He's bathing," she said. "But what do I do with his clothes?"

"I brought some nice winter breeches and a wool shirt for the boy," Miss Dandridge said. "They are in my satchel. Would you get them?"

Annie tiptoed into the bedroom, careful not to wake Mary. She reached into the satchel and dragged out the bundle of clothes. As she pulled, out fell a piece of paper. The girl bent over to retrieve it when she saw her name written in her father's hand. Looking guiltily over her shoulder to make sure Miss Dandridge wasn't watching, Annie began to read. It was apparently the page of a letter written from Patrick Henry to Miss Dandridge. "I worry about Annie," it read. "She doesn't seem like the same sweet child who came with me from Scotchtown. Last summer she begged to be allowed to stay at the tavern in Hanover—eager to work, she said. Now, she has adopted the Williamsburg sneer at everything simple. I fear that the homely virtues of faithfulness, diligence, perseverance, and kindness seem old-fashioned to her."

After reading the letter, Annie sank back on the floor, letting it drop back into the satchel. Was it true? she wondered. Had she changed so much? Looking about guiltily, Annie hopped to her feet, certain that Miss Dandridge would be coming after her in a minute. She picked up the bundle of clothes and hurried back where she found Miss Dandridge drying the little boy off. He yelled when Annie came into the room. "I don't want her to see me," he screamed. So Annie tossed the clothes to a grinning Miss Dandridge and turned her back on them.

After a few minutes, Miss Dandridge called to her. "I am not a cook," she laughed. "So I had cook prepare us a picnic supper. In fact, there is enough food here for several days. Are you hungry?"

"I'm hungry," Thomas shouted. "I'm starving. I could eat all that food," he said.

Annie scowled. "I'm not hungry," she said.

"Well, come sit with us anyway," Miss Dandridge urged. "Maybe seeing us eat will give you an appetite." She ignored Annie's downcast face. The little boy began eating as soon as the food was set before him. But Miss Dandridge reached out a restraining hand and said, "We have not prayed." Then she looked at Annie and said, "Would you ask the Lord's blessing?"

Bowing her head, Annie started praying. She found that even the simple words of thanks stuck in her throat. It had been a long time since she had prayed. Finally, she managed to croak out a few words, feeling embarrassed as she did so.

They ate and drank, and even Annie found the food too tempting to ignore. Though Miss Dandridge made pleasant conversation, Annie was distracted. She thought about her father marrying a new wife, and about her mother who had been sick and died. Why would God heal this woman and not her mother? she wondered. Her attention was brought back to the present when Thomas asked, "Is my mama going to live?"

Miss Dandridge smiled. "Such ideas you have, Thomas. Of course she's going to live."

But Annie interrupted and said out loud some of the things she had been thinking. "Sometimes mamas don't live," she said. "My mama died."

Miss Dandridge froze in her seat. Thomas's little face crumpled into tears until the older woman said bluntly, "Your mama will not die, Thomas. She's getting better. In fact, I have a surprise for you. We are going to take the two of you back to Williamsburg. We'll take our warm carriage, bundle you both up, and bring you home where your mama can get strong."

Annie threw her napkin down. "You are not God," she screamed as she rose from the table. "You don't know what will happen."

Miss Dandridge spoke calmly, but there was a no-nonsense look in her eye. "Sit down, Annie," she said. While the girl sat down, Miss Dandridge regarded Thomas, whose face showed confusion.

"Thomas, Annie is right that I am not God. I don't know all His plans. But I do know your mother is getting better. Her fever is gone, and her strength is increasing.

With care, she will be fine." The boy looked trustingly at the older woman, who turned to face Annie.

"Annie, I want you to think for a minute before you speak. Thomas needs you to tell him the truth. When your mama died, what did you learn about God?"

The question brought back a rush of memories, good and bad. Several times she began to speak, but each time Miss Dandridge said, "Have you thought it out carefully, Annie?"

Finally, the girl smiled a weak smile. She looked at Thomas and said, "I know that God, who made the heavens and the earth, does only what is right," she answered.

That answer seemed to satisfy the boy, but it didn't satisfy Annie. She worked quietly while they washed the dishes and packed away the food. Miss Dandridge tucked the little boy into his bed, and Annie was left alone in the room. For the first time she wondered where she and Miss Dandridge were going to sleep.

The older woman tiptoed out of the bedroom. "I guess we should go to bed also," she said.

"But where?" Annie asked.

"There's a barn out back. It has plenty of hay. I asked our driver to lay the blankets in the loft."

"Where will he sleep?" Annie asked.

"In the carriage, I gather."

"Won't it be cold?"

"He has blankets," she said. "Let us take a lantern and see what arrangements he's made for us."

They walked by lantern light to the barn, which was filled with sweet-smelling hay. There was a ladder up to the loft, and Miss Dandridge regarded it with amusement. "How will I climb this in my hoops," she mused aloud.

Annie laughed. "Take them off," she said. "I did."

With a feminine shrug, Miss Dandridge removed the awkward and bulky hoops and climbed the stairs to the loft. Annie, not wanting to be left alone, clambered up behind her. They found two beds made of furs and blankets on hay. The girl snuggled down in one of them, pulling the warm blankets up close to her chin and breathing deeply of the barn smells. Next to her, Miss Dandridge settled down and then blew out the lantern. Suddenly the barn was plunged into darkness.

They lay there quietly for a few minutes until Miss Dandridge said, "What else did you want to tell Thomas?"

The girl didn't answer right away. She listened to the older woman's gentle breathing and the sounds of the wind outside the barn. "I guess I wanted to tell him that things can get pretty confusing. But then I thought he was probably already confused and I didn't want to make it worse," she said.

"What do you find confusing?"

Annie thought. "I find the rules confusing," she said. "Like why do people act one way at Scotchtown and another way in Williamsburg. And I find God confusing. Why is He so far away?"

Now it was Miss Dandridge's turn to be quiet. Annie thought she had fallen asleep, but then she heard the soft voice. "I think God feels far away when we know that we've done something to displease Him," she said. "Some people live their whole lives like that. They never humble themselves and confess their sins. They pretend that they are perfect, even though they know, deep down, that they sin. We all get angry and act selfish. We all want what doesn't belong to us."

Annie shivered and pulled the cover up tighter. Then Miss Dandridge continued. "I believe what the Bible says—that if we confess our sins, Christ is faithful and just and will forgive us our sins and cleanse us from all unrighteousness."

"Even me," Annie whispered into the dark.

She felt Miss Dandridge's hand reach across and take hers. "Even you, my dear," the older woman said. "And as for manners in Williamsburg: Too many confuse money and style with good manners. Some people even think their fine clothes make them Christians. Others believe that since we have no king, we are free from all rules. They have confused liberty with license to do whatever they wish. They couldn't be more wrong. God has given us liberty so that we might do good. And we will not hold onto our liberty long if we lose our virtue. This is one of your father's greatest worries. But enough. You need your sleep, and I need mine. Good night, dear."

Annie turned her back to Miss Dandridge and

thought about the woman's words. She felt herself at a turning point. She could be self-righteous, pretending that she was perfect, or she could humble herself and admit her faults. One was the way of pride, the other the way of forgiveness. "I'm not so bad," she said at one point. But then she remembered a hundred cruel things she had done. Every time she tried shaking off the feeling and sleeping, she couldn't.

Finally, as the first rays of sun poked their way through the rafters, Annie knelt beside her blanket, confessed her sin, and begged God for forgiveness. Then she fell into a deep and dreamless slumber.

☆

Annie slept until noon. When she awoke, the bed next to her was empty. She lay there for a minute, enjoying the cold air on her face and the cozy warmth of her skin under the blanket. She knew she'd have to throw off the covers soon and make a dash for the house. Just then something pinged her on the arm. A second later, she felt a sharp pain on her toe. "What's that?" she said, bolting upright.

A giggle from down below gave her a clue. She found a little chestnut—a buckeye—near her arm and another by her foot. "I'll get you," she chuckled, pocketing both nuts. Then crawling to the edge of the loft, she peered over. No sooner had her head appeared, then she was beaned with another buckeye.

"I got you," the boy chortled, falling on his knees. "I got you good that time."

Annie let fly with one of the chestnuts she had stashed in her pocket.

"Ouch," the boy yelled, rubbing his leg where Annie had hit it.

From above, the girl grinned. "Truce?" she asked.

"All right, truce," the boy agreed, still rubbing his thigh.

Annie climbed down from the loft, straightening her wrinkled dress as she went.

"I thought you'd never wake up," Thomas said. "I only threw the buckeyes to get your attention."

"Is Miss Dandridge in the house?" Annie asked.

"Yep, she's helping Mama get dressed. We're going to Williamsburg today," the boy said, barely able to restrain his eagerness.

"Today?" Annie asked. "I best get ready. I look a mess."

"You sure do," Thomas agreed readily. "You look like you slept in those clothes."

"Well, that may be because I did," Annie replied. "Now shoo. Let me get ready."

The boy ran off with the skinny dog that Annie had seen earlier. She followed behind, shivering as she crossed the yard in her dress. In the cabin, she found a fire blazing. "Oh, it's nice in here," she said, as she stood in front of the fireplace.

"Good sleep?" Miss Dandridge inquired.

"Not hardly," Annie said, remembering the fitful night she had. "It was so odd," she continued. "After we talked, I felt so wound up. My stomach was churning and I worried over every bad thing I could ever remember doing. I felt as if I would go crazy, and when I tried to calm down or count sheep, I became even more stirred up. Finally, there seemed to be no choice. I pleaded with God to forgive me and to grant me a fresh start. And I felt a peace come over me as if He had answered. The rest of the night I slept like a baby," she said with a laugh, "that is, until Thomas woke me up."

Miss Dandridge had been listening carefully, a slow smile coming over her face. Then she bent and hugged Annie, whispering a prayer of thanksgiving to herself.

While they talked, Thomas ran back and forth from the porch. "May I take this?" he asked, holding up an old hoe.

"Let's leave that," Miss Dandridge said with a grimace.

The little boy carried the rusted tool out to the porch, but then he returned with a cracked pottery pitcher. "This is Mama's favorite," he said, holding the blue pitcher up. "We must take it with us."

Annie looked up from the satchel she was packing. "Oh, Thomas," she blurted without thinking, "that old thing is better left in a junk pile."

Tears welled up in the little boy's eyes as he appealed

to Miss Dandridge. "My daddy gave this to Mama," he said. "It is her favorite."

Annie looked humbled. "I'm sorry, Thomas," she said. "I didn't mean to hurt your feelings."

Meanwhile, Miss Dandridge looked around the room, where the piles of things that they planned to take were growing. "There is just not room in my carriage for all your belongings," she told Thomas. "Let's leave some things here so that when you come back your home will be ready for you. We'll only take what you'll need for the winter in Williamsburg."

"I guess that will be all right," the boy said. He looked around as though he were thinking of something. "I'm hungry."

"There are some apples and some cheese in the basket," Miss Dandridge answered. "I'm going to get your mama up, and then we'll be ready to go." Then, looking up, she noticed that Annie was still dressed in her same crumpled dress. "Annie, you need to change before we set out. I'll not have your father think that I neglected you."

Annie smiled. "Only made me work like a slave and sleep in a barn," she said, giving her a sly grin.

Miss Dandridge laughed. "Some people don't respond well to luxury," she said. "They need to remember who they are before God."

Annie removed her soiled dress and put on a fresh one. She moved quickly, before the little boy could do anything to embarrass her. By the time she was finished, the carriage was loaded with Mary inside on a makeshift bed. Thomas was happy to ride above with the driver, so Annie and Miss Dandridge squeezed together on the other seat.

By the time they reached Williamsburg, Annie's back and legs were sore from the bumpy trip. She was tired and glad to reach the governor's palace. When the carriage stopped and the driver helped her out, Annie saw Thomas's wide-eyed wonder at the size of the house in which she lived.

"Do you really live in that place?" the boy asked.

"Yes," she said. "And you can come visit me here."

"Really?" he asked. "You'd let me come inside?"

"Of course," the girl promised. "My friends can visit me anytime they want. And you are my friend." She reached up and shook the boy's hand, handing him the last of the buckeyes as she did so. "I'll be praying for your mama," she said.

"Me too," he answered.

Annie heard the door open behind her and saw her father's slender figure come down the stairs and stand by her side. She slipped her arm around his waist and said softly, "I'm back, Father. Annie from Scotchtown is back."

A CHRISTMAS BALL

ANNIE FOUND AN INVITATION WAITING FOR HER when she entered the house. There was to be a Christmas ball at Grace's home, and Annie and her father were invited.

"A Christmas ball?" she exclaimed when she read the neatly engraved invitation. She hadn't realized the fall had passed so quickly.

Annie ran to her closet to examine the green satin party dress that Miss Dandridge (would she ever call her Mother?) had helped her pick out. It was a beautiful gown, and Annie felt full of excitement as she thought about wearing it.

The week plodded along. But finally Friday came, and Annie was able to dress for the ball. With the maid's help, she curled her hair, making sure that the hot curling iron didn't burn it. Then, reaching into a box that she kept in her wardrobe, Annie found the tortoise shell comb that the auctioneer had given her. She had not worn it since that day.

She slipped into the dress, not even minding the feel of the hoops because the effect was so beautiful. When she twirled, her skirts billowed out around her. "Now I can use my dancing lessons," she thought as she remembered the sometimes painful sessions that she had been forced to endure.

Annie and her father pulled into the driveway at the Hall, announcing their presence with the sound of carriage bells and the twinkling of lights. They were not alone. Ahead of them were twenty carriages, each unloading its load of happy partygoers.

Annie waited impatiently for their turn with her face pressed against the carriage window. The house glowed like a lantern with the light of thousands of candles. Faint sounds of music drifted to her waiting carriage. Next to her, Patrick Henry, elegant in his satin waistcoat and breeches, tapped his foot in time to the music. "Will you dance with me?" he asked.

"I'll write you into my program," she answered playfully.

By that time their carriage had reached the veranda, and a uniformed servant opened the door and helped Annie out. She waited for her father, who guided her up the stairs and into the house. She felt overwhelmed by the press of people who crowded around, eager to shake Patrick Henry's hand. He nodded and smiled at them as he guided his daughter into the ballroom where the music played. "Let us have good music and dancing," he said to his friends. "There will be time for talk later."

Just then, Annie caught sight of Grace out of the corner of her eye. "Come with me," Grace whispered in her friend's ear. "We are having our supper in another room. Then we can join the adults for dancing."

Hand in hand, the girls skipped out of the ballroom. In a large drawing room, Annie found her friends from school, as well as many young people whom she had never met. Grace drew her into a circle of friends, and for the next few minutes, they admired each other's dresses and hair. Even Kate was there. Annie made her way next to her and said, "You look so pretty tonight."

Kate smiled shyly. "Mrs. Wythe gave me the dress. I hope it is all right?" she said, a little self-consciously.

"It looks wonderful to me."

At that moment, Grace interrupted, carrying two cups of punch. "I thought you might be thirsty," she said. "There's plenty to eat as well," she said pointing at a table laden with food.

Kate drank down her punch quickly and then giggled. "I think I'm nervous," she confided to Annie.

"I am too," Annie said. "I've never been to a ball like this either. I guess we can be nervous together."

The two girls walked toward the buffet and began filling their plates. They had just taken seats when Grace materialized again. "Here," she said. "I didn't think you could carry a plate and a cup, so I brought you some more punch."

Annie, who hadn't finished her first cup, gave Grace a funny look. But Kate accepted the fresh cup gratefully. "Thank you," she said.

The two girls settled down to eat. Kate nodded her head and tapped her toes in time with the music.

"Do you like to dance?" Annie asked.

"I never have," Kate answered. "I'm probably all left feet. But I love music, and Mrs. Wythe has been letting me play her harpsichord."

"Do you think someone will ask you to dance?" Annie asked, wondering if she would be asked by anyone other than her father.

Kate shrugged and took a last sip of her punch. "It makes me nervous just to think about it," she said.

The two girls watched the scene around them. There was some mild flirting going on between several older girls and boys. Annie watched the way the girls hid behind their fans, giggling. "If that's what it takes to get a husband," she whispered to Kate, "I guess I am doomed to never have one."

"What are you two whispering about?" Grace asked as she reappeared with two more glasses of punch. "Don't the two of you know that you are supposed to mingle, not sit alone and whisper?"

The two girls blushed guiltily. "We didn't mean to be rude," Kate apologized. "We're just finishing eating."

"Here's some punch then," Grace said. "After you finish it, you must promise me to mix with the other guests. I don't want my party to be a failure."

Kate accepted the reprimand, but Annie shook her head. "I don't know why Grace is acting like such a busybody," she said. "We aren't the only ones sitting in chairs." She felt like grumbling some more but caught herself. That's not kind, she thought.

When Kate had finished her third cup of punch, she stood up. "I'm to mingle," she said just a trifle loudly. "Wish me success." As she stood, she swayed slightly.

Annie looked at her friend curiously. "Are you feeling all right?" she asked her.

"Wonderful. Just wonderful," her friend replied. She turned abruptly and plowed into a waiter who carried a platter of cold meat pies. "Excuse me," she said as the tray tumbled to the ground, scattering food everywhere.

When Kate saw the mess she sank to her knees and began crawling around, trying to pick up the meat pies.

"I'll get them, miss," the waiter said. "You go on."

But Kate moaned. "My fault, my fault. . . ."

Annie looked around, wondering what to do. She saw Grace standing in a corner, a smug look on her face. Meanwhile, a small crowd had gathered around them. Annie heard the titters and the talk. "Girl's drunk. That's what I heard. Probably brought a flask to the party. Wait until Mrs. Wythe hears."

Without waiting to hear any more, Annie reached

down and grabbed Kate by the waist. "We need to get some air," she said quietly. "Come with me."

Kate rose to her feet unsteadily, but with Annie's arm around her, they walked to the door.

Just then, Grace called out to Annie. "Where are you going?"

"For some air," Annie answered. "My friend needs some air."

"Your friends are inside, Annie," Grace said. "Let the servants help her."

"No. Kate's my friend, and she needs me," Annie answered. Next to her, Kate giggled.

"Oh, Kate," Annie whispered. "Be quiet. Someone will hear you, and you will really be in trouble."

"But why?" Kate asked. "I'm only having fun at the party.

"But why'd you have to go and get drunk," Annie asked. "Mrs. Wythe will never forgive you."

"Drunk!" the girl said in a loud voice that Annie was sure would bring someone to investigate.

"Hush. Yes, drunk. Did you bring a flask?"

By this time, Annie's harsh words had begun penetrating Kate's drunken mind. She shook her head as though to clear it and sank down onto the floor.

Annie tightened her grip. "You can't just sit down here," she hissed. "Let's go out in the yard."

"But it's dark," Kate wailed.

"Of course it's dark," Annie said. "That's why we are going there. You don't want to be seen like this, do you?"

Kate shook her head miserably. "I don't feel that well," she moaned.

"You'll feel better when we get outdoors."

Annie pushed and pulled the other girl along the dark hallway until they reached a door leading to the backyard. Pushing it open, the girls tumbled out into the cold, black night.

"It's too cold," Kate moaned. "Oh, Annie, it's cold."

"Look, Kate," Annie said in her best matter-of-fact voice. "I'm cold also. Maybe if we go to the. . . Let's see, the kitchen will be too busy, as will the scullery. I know, the smoke house. The walls are thick, and we will be out of the wind."

Since the yard was strange, Annie wasn't sure where the smokehouse would be, but she figured it would be near, but not too near, the kitchen. Keeping in the shadows, they walked until they could see the lights of the kitchen. Finally, the two girls stumbled into the smokehouse. The room was dirty with ash, and the odor of smoked bacon and ham was overwhelming.

"I may be sick," Kate whined as she seated herself on the brick floor.

But Annie wasn't paying any attention. "I just can't figure out how this happened," she said. "What did you have to drink tonight?"

"Just the punch that Grace brought to me," Kate sniffled.

"Grace Jones," Annie said with disgust. "That is too low." She suddenly remembered the smug look she had seen when Kate bumped into the waiter. "She must have mixed something in the punch."

"But didn't you drink the punch?" Kate asked.

Annie shook her head. "I didn't like the taste of it," she confessed.

"And I drank three glasses," Kate moaned. "No, four. I drank one of yours, as well."

From outside the smokehouse, they heard the sudden sound of footsteps and then the heavy door creaked open. Before either girl had a chance to be afraid, a voice said, "So that's where you ran off to."

Kate screamed, but Annie stared white-faced at the coarse, whiskered man who now stood about two feet from her. He peered at her from beady eyes. Out of the corner of his mouth he spat a stream of brown liquid that splashed on Kate's white dress sending the girl into a new round of wailing. Annie knew she had seen him before.

"Who are you?" Annie asked.

"I think you know me," he growled. "I know who you are."

The man drew closer, and Annie screamed as she recognized the auctioneer. He clapped a rough hand over her mouth and snarled, "Shut up. I'll see your father, the fancy governor, pay a pretty penny for your return."

Keeping his hand pressed tightly over her mouth, the man lifted her as though she were nothing more than a sack of feathers. Then, as the lantern light glowed softly on Annie's hair, the man saw the tortoiseshell comb. "It's a beautiful thing, isn't it?" he said as he yanked it out of her hair and stuffed it in his pocket.

☆

Ignoring Kate, who lay moaning on the floor, the man pushed through the door and stumbled with Annie into the darkness. She struggled against him, but he easily subdued her with his massive arm. He squeezed harder until she thought he might squeeze the breath out of her. Still, she struggled. "There's no point in all that wiggling," the man said. "Ain't no one going to hear you. My horse is just behind those trees there. We'll be gone, and there won't be no hope for you, unless your pa wants to pay a ransom. Like that nice comb. I got that from your pa. I bet you didn't know that."

Annie stopped wiggling, wanting him to continue his story. As she relaxed, so did he. "Yep. Course, I didn't know it were your pa. I saw a broken-down carriage and ransacked a trunk. Didn't know 'til later that your pa were in it—could have held him for ransom if I had. But now I got the daughter, and my guess is the governor will pay quite a bit to get you back."

While he talked, the man slowed his pace, stopping every several feet to catch his breath. He cursed softly.

Though she was light, she made an awkward bundle because her hoop skirts kept getting in the way. He loosened his arm as one of the wire hoops bit into his flesh, and Annie took that opportunity to free her arm from his grasp. Now, instead of both arms being tightly held against his body, one of her arms hung free. The man didn't notice.

"We're almost there," he muttered to himself. Surreptitiously, Annie reached into the bad man's pocket and felt for the comb he had stuffed there. Grasping it tightly in her hand, she drew it out. Then, with the courage that comes from desperation, she jammed the comb into the man's ear until he screamed in pain. He opened his arms and dropped the girl, who ran clumsily away. When she had put about twenty yards between them, she screamed as loudly as she could.

From down the hill Annie heard voices, and she screamed louder. Behind her she heard heavy footsteps, so she kept running, blinded by the tears that flooded her eyes.

"Whoa," a voice said, as two strong arms grabbed her. Annie swung her fist until it connected with the face of the man who held her. "Ouch," he said. "Here, perhaps you'd better take her. After all, she's your daughter."

Hearing those words, Annie stopped her kicking and screaming. "Father," she said.

"What happened to you, Annie?" he asked as he folded her into an embrace.

"Oh, Father. That disgusting man. He's the one who

robbed the coach. And he's the one who tried to grab me at the fair. And he's the one at the auction. . . ."

"What auction? What fair? What man? This is all confusing. Let's go back to the house and hear this story."

"But Father, he's getting away," Annie cried. In the distance, they could hear the scrambling of feet. "He said he has a horse there."

By now they were close to the stable. "Round up some men and we'll go after him," a young man told a groom. He rubbed his bruised jaw ruefully. Annie looked at him, and the young man smiled. "You certainly know how to find excitement, Annie Henry," he said. "But perhaps your father needs to teach you that the quiet life has its virtues as well."

"Did I hurt you?" she asked.

"I would never admit that you did," he answered, climbing on his horse.

When the posse had ridden off, Annie turned to her father, who held her arm tightly. He said, "That Spencer Roane is a fine young man. I'd be proud to have him for a son." And for some reason Annie blushed.

☆

Later, after they had rescued poor Kate from the smokehouse where she had fallen asleep, a group gathered at the governor's mansion to discuss the night's events. The two girls, Kate and Annie, were a mess. Their dresses were soot-covered, and Annie's was torn from her run through the trees. Their hair was bedraggled, and Kate complained of a splitting headache.

Word came that the outlaw had been apprehended and now sat in the public jail. Mrs. Wythe came to collect Kate. Instead of being angry, she winked at Annie and said, "It's that Grace Jones, not my good Kate, who should be punished."

Miss Dandridge sipped a cup of warm herb tea. "I can't get over the lawlessness of some men," she said for the fifth time.

Taking her hand in his, Patrick Henry said, "We shouldn't be surprised. Sin lurks in all our hearts. But I pray that God would restrain evil, and do a work of reformation among us. If we are not a virtuous people, we won't long be a free people."

Then, looking at his daughter, he said, "I hope you've learned your lesson about using my position to gain favors."

She nodded, suppressing a yawn. "I didn't know it was your comb, Father."

"But that isn't the point. I bought that comb for Miss Dandridge, it is true. By accepting it from the auctioneer, you brought into question my integrity. You made it seem as though the man had to pay a bribe to get into my good favor."

"I'm sorry, Father," Annie answered.

"Then I'll say no more."

A WEDDING

ONE DAY IN EARLY JANUARY, ANNIE AND MISS Dandridge sat sewing in the parlor. A huge fire roared in the fireplace; outside, several inches of new snow blanketed the ground.

"I remember when Patsy was preparing for her wedding," Annie said, thinking back two years.

"I wish I had met your sister," Miss Dandridge said. "We live too far from your family, I think."

"But they will come here for the wedding, won't they?" Annie asked.

Miss Dandridge set down her sewing on the settee. She stared dreamily at the fire. When she didn't answer, Annie looked up from her own stitching. "They will be at the wedding?" she repeated with a touch of anxiety.

Miss Dandridge shook her head as though chasing away cobwebs. "I'm sorry, dear," she said. "I wasn't paying attention. Of course they'll be at the wedding." But then her face took on a sad look.

"What is troubling you?"

"You may think I'm silly," the older woman said sheepishly.

"I won't think that of you," Annie answered with a smile.

"Do you think your father would mind being married at Scotchtown?"

"Scotchtown?" Annie asked. "But why? You have the beautiful mansion here, and all your friends are here. Why would you want to go to Scotchtown?" As she talked, Annie paced back and forth in front of the fireplace, her skirts making a noisy swishing sound as she passed.

"Annie, sit down," Miss Dandridge said, a bit impatiently. "Your pacing is making me nervous."

Annie blushed and sat down. Miss Dandridge had never snapped at her like that. For several minutes both ladies were silent. Then Miss Dandridge said apologetically, "I'm sorry. I am all a flutter over this wedding."

Again the room was quiet. Only the ticking of the clock broke the silence before the older woman spoke. "I'd like nothing more than to be married at Scotchtown," she said. "That home has been such a big part of your family's life. . . . I guess I'd feel more a part of the family if our wedding took place there."

Annie thought about that for a minute. "And you

wouldn't mind not being married in the Governor's Palace?" she asked.

"Not at all," Miss Dandridge replied. "Your father has only one more year as governor, and then we'll leave Williamsburg for good. This is not our home."

"But what about all the people you know here?"

"Annie, most of these people are not friends. They are political friends or allies. They like your father because he is the governor. But in Hanover, he has true friends. Some were his friends when to most of the world he was a failure."

"What does Father say?"

Now it was Miss Dandridge's turn to blush. "I haven't asked him. I'm afraid maybe he has his heart set on being married here, and I'm willing to do whatever will make him happy."

"That's silly," Annie said. "I bet Father doesn't care. Why don't you just tell him what you told me," she added.

"I will," Miss Dandridge promised. "But would you do me a favor first? Will you find out your father's thinking on this subject?"

"Do you mean right now?" Annie asked.

"Well, it doesn't have to be this instant," Miss Dandridge said. "But . . ."

By this time Annie was on her feet and at the parlor door. "Why don't you send for tea," she said. "I won't be but a minute."

She took the stairs two at a time, despite her skirts.

Outside her father's door, she paused to catch her breath. Then she knocked.

"Come in," he called.

She found him sitting at his writing desk, a stack of letters before him. "I find this writing to be tedious," he said. "I wish you would make progress in your penmanship so that you could do some of this for me."

Annie looked shamefaced. Despite her best efforts and the patient instruction of Miss Dandridge, her handwriting was still plagued by ink splotches. Annie sat on the edge of her father's tall, canopy bed. He turned in his chair until he was facing her.

"Well, Daughter?" he asked.

"I wanted to know where you were getting married?" Annie blurted.

"That's Miss Dandridge's decision," he answered, turning back to his letters.

"Wait," Annie said. "Do you not care where the wedding takes place?"

"I've assumed it would be here at the Palace, or maybe at the Bruton Parish Church. But why not ask Dorothea?"

"Why not Scotchtown?" Annie asked, looking intently at her father while she said it.

Her question took him by surprise. He rubbed his jaw as though thinking about it for the first time. "I couldn't ask Dorothea to get married in the country," he said finally.

"But is that what you'd want?" Annie persisted.

"It would certainly make things easier," he said. "There

would be no need for the whole family to come to Williamsburg, and we could just stay for the summer. We must not remain in this dank town during the wet summer months." Then he shook his head. "No. I couldn't ask her to make that sacrifice."

Annie hopped down from the bed. She placed a kiss on her father's cheek before saying "thank you" and skipping out. Her father stared at her retreating figure, a puzzled look on his face.

Back downstairs, Annie drank the cup of tea that Miss Dandridge held out to her. Despite the older woman's eager expression, she kept silent, enjoying her chance to tease. Miss Dandridge was too well-bred to beg, so the two drank their tea in silence until Annie tired of the game.

"Father says it's up to you," she said finally.

Hearing those words, Miss Dandridge's expectant smile fell. "That means he'd prefer the Governor's Palace, doesn't it?" she asked.

"He said. . ." Annie tried to hide her smile but failed. "He said it would be more convenient at Scotchtown, but he couldn't ask you to make that sacrifice."

Suddenly, Miss Dandridge smiled. "That's fine," she said. "I choose to be married at Scotchtown. Now to tell your father and write to Patsy." She paused for a minute. Worry furrowed her brow. "Will Patsy think it too much trouble?" she said.

"You don't know Patsy," Annie said with a grin. "She

loves a good party—and you will give her great pleasure preparing for it."

"Good," Miss Dandridge answered. "Then I must write to her and ask."

☆

In May, 1777, Annie returned triumphantly to Scotchtown with her father and Miss Dandridge. The house was filled, not only with the Henry family, but with the many guests who had come from all around for the wedding.

The house was noisy and filled with laughter. Annie's brothers and sisters demanded to hear all the news from Williamsburg, and there was much bragging and teasing. Several days after arriving, Annie wandered outside near her mother's lilac tree, which was laden with sweet-smelling blooms. She sat on the bench near the tree, glad to be alone, if only for a few minutes.

"You'd like Miss Dandridge," she whispered out loud, as though talking to her mother. "She's kind and good, and she loves Father very much. She even likes me," Annie said shyly. She hugged herself with happiness. Annie looked awkwardly around her to make sure no one was listening. "I love you, Mama," she whispered. "I feel so happy because I love Miss Dandridge also."

☆